IDENTITY QUEST

The Dark Path

About The Author

Reynold Sibanda is a Zimbabwean writer in his twenties from the city of Mutare. *IDENTITY QUEST The Dark Path* marks his debut novel.

Also By the Same Author

LIFE AS WE LIVE IT: Short Stories Collection

IDENTITY QUEST

The Dark Path

REYNOLD SIBANDA

Darling Kind Publishing

An Imprint of TatendaCharlesMunyuki Publishing

IDENTITY QUEST: The Dark Path

First published in Zimbabwe in 2017.
Darling Kind Publishing
an imprint of Tatenda Charles Munyuki Publishing.

Copyright © Reynold Sibanda 2017.
Cover Illustration Copyright© Straightline Designz 2017.
Cover illustration by Straightline Designz 2017.

The moral rights of the author have been asserted.

ISBN   978 0 7974 7785 8

Printed and bound by Darling Kind Publishing,
Harare, Zimbabwe.
darlingkindp@live.com

facebook.com/tcmpublishingzim

ACKNOWLEDGEMENTS

Special thanks to my family who never ceased to stand beside me despite the fall backs that I had in trying to write this book, they believed in me even when I fell and stood by me through thick and thin. Ideas were constantly whispered into my ears even when I felt too tired to write. That is the spirit of inspiration guys. I love you all, my Mom Ellen, my sisters Eunice and Sibusisiwe, and my brothers, Felix, Thulani, Regnald, Ronald, Richard, Ndabaezinhle and little Kiki. I am blessed to have such a wonderful and loving group around me that I am glad to call family.

Many thanks to my friend and typist Peter, whose round the clock typing made this work possible, without forgetting my friend Simbarashe Bosha, whose whispered ideas, mixed up as they were, contributed much to the creation of this book.

I acknowledge the heavy involvement of Simbarashe Mwaxx Mwanaka, a good friend and sometimes rival, whose ideas were stepping-stones in the course of writing this book and who also contributed by agreeing to write the foreword of this book even on short notice.

I also thank my schoolmates, Paul Mao Maorera, Constantine 'Con Con' Mudanda, Lloyd Tiger Tigere, Tatenda Kedha Warara, David Diva Pfumvuti, Livingstone Ngisiladen Mangisi, Edwin Koax Makokoro, Liberty Chikosha, Tinotenda Zhacks Zhakata, Tafadzwa Chamhamha Dzomonda, Kumbirai Kays Katsande, Biggie Mandidewa, Leonard Dzik Dzik Dzikira, Junior Jujuju Mazhomba and Vincent Vinnie Chimbeke only to mention a few for the inspiration and flattery without which I wouldn't have written this book. You are such a wonderful team guys and I thank the Lord for putting our destinies on a collision course for the best.

Friendship, I discovered is a two way street, a vine that bears both life and death, for there were other friends whom I will mention not on this platform, but maybe in times to come, whose criticism was meant to bring me down, meant to snuff out the fires of my dreams, but it is people like Manbee and Mao who showed me that in life we might not be tied together by blood or such, but still there exists in this world other bonds that are equally strong and long lasting as the bonds of blood and that blood is not always thicker than water. Thumbs up guys!

I also hereby thank all the children of the streets who secretly and unknowingly inspired most of the scenes in this book, those children who follow a sordid, terrifying and lonely path in life, eating where the dogs eat, with nothing to hold on to, no future to run towards and no parent to love and hold them. Remember there is always life after death and there is always light at the end of the tunnel. Don't lose hope for all shall be well. Wherever you are, my heart reaches out to you guys.

Reynold Sibanda 2017

A MESSAGE TO HUMANITY

There are children who receive the wrath of all seasons of the year like trees, with no shelter or protection, children who lie where the dogs lie and feed where the dogs feed. There are children who have no parent to run home to and no one to compliment them in happier times which in their world seldom comes, children who wish to die, but cannot for their time is not yet right, their destination is not yet ready in the heavens above. Young souls whose cries go unchecked until they run out of tears, children whose greatest wish is a hot meal which is in their minds just, but a fantasy, a belief that maybe in the life after, in the world beyond, might be fulfilled.

There are a wrathful group of children haunting the streets, born innocent, peaceful and vulnerable, hardened by the streets and violent by exposure to a sinful world, a world they have been exposed to long before their time. These people grow even more irritable with the passage of time until they are just one person, until they speak with only one voice, *the voice of rage.*

There are children out there on the streets who have since begun to doubt the existence of a Merciful God because from birth they have not seen what others saw and so will never be what others are. Don't judge them by who they are, but by the circumstances that lead them to where they are and by the atrocities people daily commit upon them to shape their destiny.

People must not be judged in life by who they are or who they become, for one will never know the wars that were fought for them to be where they are or become who they are. For some it is choice and for some fate, for some it is destiny, but it is for the unfortunate majority that my heart reaches out, it is for the unlucky population that my heart weeps. It is for those whose destiny was shaped out by other people, whose attention I seek.

There are people who were ill fated on birth by forces beyond their control and born blind or crippled and those born with little intellect, but it is those who were born blessed, but whose destiny was predetermined by people with whom they trust who cry the most. For these people put their trust in parents and relatives who never dreamt of a world beyond, where the child might become a powerful someone. These people confine the lives of an individual to what they themselves grew up like and in most times even try to reduce the children's privileges to something even less.

Many children have accepted this, the life thrust upon them by parents and guardians, but it is those of a rebellious nature who find their way out of the homes to land on the not so prestigious home called *the streets*. These children some may say, are weak in mind or are thoughtless, but personally I don't know what to call them for only a few understand or will ever get to really know what goes on in the minds of such individuals.

There are others, the under-privileged who lose either or both parents to the call of time and are left in the care of a less motherly or fatherly relative who take the opportunity of being in care as that of having an instrument to abuse, whip and use at will. It is to everyone on the streets that many label as thieves, prostitutes, destitutes, muggers, but instead many of these children will have no evil in mind other than just a silent plea to the general public for a decent meal, sometimes uttered out, but with no confidence.

It is for these children who have no control of their destiny, who had fate thrust upon them that I cry out to the Merciful one for pity and whom I many times shed a silent tear for, for if I die today, will my children also follow this lonely and sad path? If so, then may the Lord bless me enough to see them through this phase in life. May God bless the children of the streets and those with whom their lives interlink so that they are seen not with eyes of hatred, but just as a child less fortunate than the rest, but who has equal abilities for goodness as the average child with proper shelter.

It is time that humanity come together in the fight against child abuse whether physical, psychological emotional or sexual. It is time the average parent treats the *children of the streets* in the same manner as they treat the *children on the streets*. Let the world open their eyes and see the beauty in them and not only the ugliness. Together we can make a difference to them, together we can give a home and save a soul.

It is to all who feel for the children of the streets that I also dedicate this book and my love.

Reynold Sibanda 2017

FOREWORD

Nothing builds a more dangerous person than shuttered hope, rejection and lack of security. The proportional addition of frustration builds an even more bizarre world that is degraded of any humility and void of humanity. The result is the emergence of a desolate universe in which the feeling of closeness and similarity to a True God is rapidly and exponentially vanishing like in the ancient biblical cities of Sodom and Gomorrah.

While the production of such a universe seems to be a production of Sci-fi, or a blend of Greek folklore and the Armageddon speculations, it is within our midst. All you have to do is to get into the streets at night and experience a world that exist in the world that we live in, the world of the street children.

Such a pandemonium that is felt by the street urchins is the one that caught the eye of the author of this book, an emotional friend of mine who was greatly touched by innocent souls already serving a hell term on Mother Earth while the majority turn a blind eye.

Regardless of the global statistics that seem to suggest that a score of human rights organisations are doing a plausible job in trying to make sure that the life of every individual on planet Earth is made easy, a gaze into the deep reality produces conflicting visions.

There are still children roaming the streets at night and during the day, not for the pleasure of it, but because to them it is home. With the passage of each calendar day, they are hardened to beings less human, thieves, robbers, prostitutes and a whole host of other nasty characters not so lovable and welcome to the society that we live in. They fall prey to traffickers who come under the guise of human right activists and are subject to all forms of abuse, with no one to turn to, for who in this world can take the word of a street kid seriously?

The characters in this book leaped from the pages and moved me into a terrifying reality as I perused the pages and realised what a terrible world existed around me which I was just too blind to notice only until this book. I then began to take notice of these children and how they live, monuments of a blank stolen future with experiences summing up the definition of hopelessness and nothingness. Even I cannot help feeling pity for these children and their wandering minds, more lost than the wandering bodies. I hope this book will move a soul to make a difference for these children and the world that they walk through. Well done Rey for bringing this book to life.

Simbarashe SJM Mwanaka 2017

For my family, to fulfil dreams nurtured from childhood's early hour. For all my friends, to bring back those childhood memories that remind me of the merry old days, a time long past, but still cherished.

And for my Dad, Reggie Sibanda, even beyond the grave, in that land of no return, you are still the best Dad. Blessed be you who shall be remembered always, with love

The first thing she felt as she read the letter was panic, then fear, then anger. It was a pure unholy anger. It was anger on herself, anger on her daughter and anger on her husband. It was anger on the birth registration system, which to her had delayed her registration process. It was just an unselective anger on all of them. Anger on the whole ministry and anger on the fat potbellied man who sat behind the counter at those offices who seemed never to care about the children with him he had been assigned to help acquire births.

Her mind kept telling her that it was an impossible scenario yet the evidence of her own eyes would not enlighten her grieving heart.

Was it a dream?

Was the girl just joking with her mother and pretending?

But jokes of this nature were nothing near the personality of the girl in question. They were never a part of the girl whom from the start was unlike any other, having been bred in her own unique way by a stepfather twice removed from the world of fatherhood in a generation, which needed good fathers. The stepfather was a father to whose mind a stepdaughter was something inhuman, an instrument to manipulate and to abuse, an object at his disposal to use and spit at.

The single bed that took up most of the space in the room hadn't been slept in or if it had, then all trace of the occupation was gone, both the tell-tale signs and the occupant vanished without trace as if they were some object in the Bermuda triangle where anything could actually vanish without a trace.

The bed was neatly made just as it had been the previous night when she had entered the room to reprimand her daughter for disrespecting the stepfather, the man who had married her after her first marriage had failed.

The earthen floor had been swept clean and the few

clothes that had been her only loved belongings in her adolescent years had been neatly packed and placed in a corner, pieces of clothing which meant nothing to a girl of her time in any other area of the country, but to the daughter had represented the world of nice clothes and Christmas wear. These were clothes the girl had cherished and always took time to just look at them to assure herself they were still there, the ways of a girl born in the remote areas.

The small piece of paper that she had picked and now held limply in her hand had been placed where it could never be missed. It was scrawled in the writing of her barely literate fifteen-year-old daughter, the words simple yet heavy, the words that would haunt a mother for months to come, the voice of rage.

Dear Mother

I am sorry that I didn't have the strong to bid you bye in a way that is fit for a daughter to her mother. What you told me yesterday about never getting me a birth certificate left me with no option but to go out into the world and try to secure an identity for myself among those who care or who may even just pretend to care. As you said I am a disgrace to you and am not good to use your surname. Thanks for bringing me into the world. I took only what belongs to me. Don't try to find me because the moment I stepped out I became no face, no name and above all wild.

Till we meet again

Yours No Identity Daughter

CHAPTER ONE

The girl moved as silently as she could through the forest, her heart beating wildly against her chest to the point of nearly paralysing her. The lump in her throat was threatening to choke her and made it difficult for her to swallow. She had to open her mouth to breathe freely. The possibility of being followed by her stepfather kept her going even in the middle of the tangled forests of the farmlands most of which were wild. Her name was Panaka, a budding girl in her early adolescent years.

According to the standards of the farm, she was good looking, dark in complexion, the kind of complexion that might have brought about the old adage that *black is beauty*. She had a bright liquid fire in each of her eyes, which had begun to get dull because of the many sad episodes life and brought into the story of her life.

She was slightly cross eyed, something that gave her the appearance of always looking aside each time she was looking at something, but only a few ever talked about her disability if this was anything near to it.

The animals of summer were singing and screeching in the night as they had always done, unknowingly adding fear to some little girl's mind and eeriness to a night that was itself dark and threatening, with the promise of yet another downpour that would bring the little town closer and closer to the brink of yet another year of floods.

Floods, it seemed, the people in the area had become used to and what everyone hoped for was that they wouldn't be the floods that had destroyed the world at some point back in time, the biblical floods that made father Noah a hero in the eyes of men and brought man and animal together.

The issue of floods or the spectacles of nature were nothing near what went on in Panaka's mind as she moved in the wild. The only thing she wanted to do was to put as much distance as she could between herself and the house that she had decided not to call home. She had no idea where she was headed and did not want to stop. The only things she had taken were the few clothes she had bought with her own hard-earned cash, money she had got by working at the farm during her school holidays and weekends and nothing of what her parents had bought for her.

She did not want them to think she depended much on them. She wanted to disconnect herself as much as possible from the stepfather who took her for granted and from a mother who was so blinded by love and marriage, blinded by her very much lasting and enduring loyalty or was it even worship for this man that she could do anything for her husband at the expense of her own daughter, at the expense of her own blood. Panaka felt that it wasn't even love that bound her mother to the man, but something else, something sinister or maybe trying to be like everyone else, married and living with a man. *Or was it to cure the pain and fill the void left by Panaka's father?*

So how far true was the statement that, *Blood was always thicker than water?*

Did it ever come into play under these circumstances or love was thicker than anything else?

Was love such a strong emotion such as to erase every other aspect of human relations?

Was it so enjoyable to the extent that one could give up everything else, even their very own lives in the quest for it?

Was this emotion, this love so very enjoyable such that one could die for it?

Was it so powerful an emotion that one could cry for it like many older girls always did after rejection?

She had never fallen in love before and always thought how people could actually love anyone so much, but she doubted she could give up her own children in the wake of love or if she ever would, then God should strike her dead or curse her and whoever would be her accomplice to the grave.

Her mind went back to her present situation. Being caught now meant a heavy beating by both her parents and who knew maybe even some home imprisonment for some time and that was a fact. It had happened several times and she knew this one more time would do no difference and during those times, school she had missed also.

School, her stepfather said was only for those men who wished to live beyond the world that God had created for them.

These children of your time suffer all this time going to school and such because they are not satisfied with whom they are. They are men, but wish to be something more than mere men. They wish to be gods,' were the words he always said each time the subject of school was raised. *'You go to school only to be able to count money you get as wages and to learn to sign against your name anything more than that is not for farm girls like you to do as such. Once a girl from the farms go beyond the world that was designed for her, once she attempts to pursue this so called education much she becomes a rebel to her husband, an outcast of tradition.'*

Whether this was a result of the beer he drank on a daily basis or the marijuana he smoked daily, or even by a heart that was barren and void of care, Panaka did not know or even care. What mattered was that by the way he said it, it was clear he meant every word of it. These were not words a father could say to a daughter, but sometimes Panaka did not blame him. He had never seen the doors of any school for he had been raised in destitution by his grandparents. He was to her a living testimony that most of those who grew up under extremely shabby and abusive environs grew and ended up taking their fury onto the world and its inhabitants. Most of these people would have grown up with the belief that it was more natural to do bad than good for in their minds would be very little memories of the good that had been done to them, but of the bad there will be endless memories.

So who was to blame, the bad people or their backgrounds? Was it always that the guardians be blamed for the bad that people do?

Was it the same God she worshiped that had created men of this nature, men of a rough persuasion?

Her mind wandered back to the present, to the rugged path she was following now that led to the great Nyamauru River and being the time of the year as it was she could hear that part of it that made it a river, the heavy roar of water as it made contact with the banks on its journey to the unknown distant lands where legend had it that there was so much water to sink a whole country and water enough to float a very big boat.

Rumour had it those distant, large bodies of water harboured creatures that were half human and half fish which they called *mermaids* which had supernatural powers and creatures so big they could swallow a whole bus. Their teacher had said that boats as big as their school or even bigger could float on these waters and everyone wanted to see these waters, but none was prepared to meet the creatures.

Whether this was true or not, Panaka did not dwell much on this thought, for there was a journey to be planned and it was to be done in her very head, that head many teachers had deemed dull, the very head the stepfather had said was good for nothing, the same head that failed to work out very simple mathematical sums because it was occupied with several other things was at this time being subjected to a whole new challenge. The challenge of making a life changing decision.

Was it this time that her mind was waiting for in order to

prove its worth, to make the kind of decisions life required of her?

It was at such moments that people found the anarchy that made them adults, when the decisions of life and death lie on the shoulders of those who have always in their lives been the weaklings and were spoon fed by their mothers in the nests and when responsibility loomed, they hunted for reasons to evade it only to discover that reason isn't an option that time around.

The sound in the night was several times more pronounced than she knew it to be in the daytime to the point of nerve wrecking and the girl found her teeth chattering and to her dismay found that her body was trembling, vibrations whose presence in a human body was associated with uncertainty, insecurity and above all, fear.

Something moved to her side and she jumped, clutching the small bag tighter to her budding bosom which back at the farms had begun to attract several lustful eyes from some would be suitors and she quickened her pace to match her pulse. Sweat broke on her forehead and she wiped it off with the back of her hand.

She was approaching the river now and in her mind, she played her plan beyond the river. In her bag she had around fifteen dollars, an amount that would get her into the Mutare Township where she had been only several times and from there she wanted to go to Harare the big city where legend had it that the streets were inhabited by children with no identities, but who lived large despite their fate.

The children, legend had it, had forged a relationship among themselves and though they were not bound by blood, they were bound by bonds of comradeship that were equally strong, the bonds of sharing the same plight, bonds of sharing the same pain, the same bonds that made gangsters the united teams they are, the bonds of a common cause which no one outside their circles could understand unless one got to walk down their road, the road less travelled.

Panaka knew that her money, well managed, could get her there and she would live with the other children on the streets and forge bonds and relations that would transcend time and maybe continue into the next world. The white waters of the river came into sight frothing immensely in the dark night and the white of the froth on the banks clinging to trees like some foam of the *gods*. The water came up the banks to the tree line and with a heavy heart, Panaka sank up to her knees as realisation dawned upon her and not without pain. The river was flooded.

It always happened in life she had heard many say, that it is always at a time that the wheels of fortune have stopped spinning in one's favour that all misfortune descend unto a person and back then she had dismissed it as mere philosophy. *What was she to do now for she could not turn back at this point?* The bridge was rather too far to try to make a go for it.

For some time, she sat there, tears of frustration rolling down her cheeks pondering on what her next move could be. Decisively she stood up. She would make a go for it no matter what. There was no going back now. She would work her way through the flooded river following the boulders that were not visible now, but having grown in the area she knew they were there. It was what people called experience, knowing in detail an area because of going through it repeatedly, that marvellous thing that distinguished people. An attribute born of numerous experiments. *Only those who experimented were prone to be experienced.*

Taking a deep sigh, Panaka decisively stood up and clutched her bag tightly in the right hand whilst she removed the sandals from her feet and placed them in the bag and her left hand gathered her long skirts up to her thighs.

Uncertainly she tested her grip on the bag and felt satisfied she was ready to cross the great river beyond which lay the township and probably even her future, a future that she already found herself fantasizing about.

Carefully, she stepped into the water saying a silent prayer. With studied chameleon steps, she moved through the water until she reached the first boulder that marked the normal level of the water before the rains. She was now knee deep in water.

Carefully and with the skill of one having grown up in the rural areas, she made her way across the river careful not to lift her legs too much in case she lost her balance. She made good progress and halfway through the river, the water was up her thighs and she made it past.

She was nearing the other bank now and her pace increased. The bank was now several metres away and getting closer with each coming step when she moved her right leg and something stuck her left leg from beneath the water.

She lost her balance and stumbled, arms flailing hit the water, the bag thrown from her hand to land with a small splash somewhere in the darkness, the last trace of the bag, a sound that was as if the bag and its contents were bidding farewell to her in a way that was near mockery.

Her head went under, but only for the briefest of moments and as someone who had learned to swim in the dark murky waters of this river she quickly broke the surface again and gasped for breath like a fish that had just been landed by a tired fisherman even as her hands began to move in the act of swimming, the urge to survive that existed in every being all too obviously aroused in her but the gods of the river it seemed were either testing her or were up against her.

The current swept at her and she found herself being swept downstream against her will. For the first time since leaving home, she felt truly frightened and she screamed, only for water to flow into this new, small opening at a pace that was frightening and she quickly clamped her mouth shut.

So this was how it was like to die in the water, she thought now, the spirit willing to escape to the safety of the banks, but the strength of the flesh rather too weak to overcome the might of a thousand streams all interwoven to empty into the great river that was Nyamauru whose strength increased downstream as a new stream joined in and then she was no longer thinking as she felt herself sinking into a blackness that she devised to be the final night, the foretold darkness of death under whose power light was forever defeated.

Pain brought Panaka back to the world of the living, that conscious world in which there are little excuses for the delay of misfortunes, the world of reality. It was a searing pain all over her body that made her wince. She opened her eyes as she heard the roaring sound of the river around her and reality struck hard and terrifying. She was caught in the branches of a huge tree that had fallen part way into the river. The huge branches must have jarred her body with the impact of the current and that explained the pain, but she had no time for that. She had to get out of the water. *But how?* Then as if a powerful god had come for her, the solution revealed itself. She would simply climb the tree trunk and follow it out to the bank. She moved her body that ached all over and cried out loud as sharp protrusions where the branches had snapped tore at her numb skin, creating regions of open skin from which blood flowed out, but she continued on up the branches and crawled along the tree trunk with the clumsiness that would be a shame to the ape community which thrived on tree climbing.

When at last she reached the banks, she threw herself to

the ground and lay there for some time, shivering uncontrollably. By then the Eastern horizon was lighted up in the orange glow of approaching day.

It was then that the irony of her situation struck her, severely. She had lost the bag that had the money. With painful realisation, Panaka found out that her situation was nearly hopeless now. She was wet and bruised all over and she felt hurt and sore. She looked around her.

She was under the cover of some thick brambles, which prevented her from seeing a complete view of the sky above.

'I am going to crawl out of here,' she told herself even as her senses began to drown in a pool of their own which seemed to suck her to the very bottom with a power that was terrifying and she blacked out, unwillingly sucked into the swirling subconscious undercurrents.

When again she regained consciousness she could tell the sun was in the middle of its journey to the heavens because of the brightness that blinded her and the first thing she felt was the hollow pit that had formed in her stomach. It was a painful hollowness that she had never believed could be so severe.

She moved all her limbs, testing for serious injury and they complied in a way that made her conclude nothing was broken. Painfully, she propped herself up against the trunk to a sitting position calculating her chances now. The combination of the afternoon heat and an empty stomach was always very powerful and by and by, her eyes became heavy until they became too much for the little energy that remained in her muscles and again she lapsed into unconsciousness.

CHAPTER TWO

The bite of mosquitoes woke her up, their singing in her ears irritated her, and she swung her hand in reflex to ward them off. She jerked up, tried to stand up, and banged her head against the branches above her head knocking sense into her and she remembered her predicament.

It was dark now and she had to move. The cold was chilling her down to the bone. Peering closely in the darkness, she crawled out of the mesh of branches and soon was free and as someone who had haunted the farms for long, she quickly figured out where she was. She was about three kilometres from the dirt road that led to the township. She was going to make for it no matter the situation and she walked headed for it.

There was no marked path that led straight to the road from her position and she moved over uneven ground, her unprotected feet being terrorised by the unfriendly ground and the stubs of burnt grass, which were the remnants of the fires of spring that always preceded summer. One thing though that was to Panaka's advantage was that her feet were not the soft tender feet of the city dwellers that would have been by now paralysed.

The feet of someone who had walked the length and breadth of the farms barefooted, feet whose skin could not be penetrated so easily.

It was a wonder how sometimes we go through life in uncertain ways, grieving and moaning on the way we are bred and how hopeless our situations could be, unknowing that life is just, but a phase of preparation, preparing men for the final test in life and to Panaka it was as if the whole period of walking around with no shoes, poverty it might have been to her, but she had been unknowingly preparing for this day the final test and she walked easily through the hostile ground.

How was she going to get to the township now? She had no money in her pocket, not even a dollar and now without any shoes she could not go to anyone for help. But first, so that she couldn't lose her way she had to reach the main dirt road first and there she was headed.

When she reached the dirt road, her stomach was completely empty now and she was trembling from cold. She took the road walking in the direction of town, constantly peering back, on the lookout for the creatures of the night, jumping at the slightest sound and moaning, sounds that came unwillingly from between closed lips.

Hunger she discovered was an element whose severity could never been clearly explained to one who had never seen its extremes. For now, Panaka's stomach was churning in a way that seemed to squeeze tears from somewhere in her body and she found herself crying even as she walked on, unable to stop not wanting to return home, for the grievances of several years could not be redeemed by a single day of hunger. The fires of years of abuse could not be extinguished by tears from a single night of hunger.

She had walked for several kilometres when she saw from a distance the lights of the town, those bright coloured lights that resembled nothing Panaka had seen in real life, but had only marvelled at as she browsed through some foreign magazines the teacher had shown them at school. The combination of all brightly coloured lights was not only dazzling, but had never been more clearly exemplified.

The lights seemed to give new strength to Panaka whose pace increased as she walked the last distance towards the town where she was going to face the unknown. It was there that she hoped the journey of her life would start, where the wheels of the train towards her destiny would be set in motion.

She knew that it was in these last few days, these last few hours that the real journey of her life had been launched, in these hours that both the inner and outer limits of what was to be her fortune had been determined.

She reached the outskirts of town at the same time that the sun was beginning its tour of the earth below. The few people she met looked at her with unconcealed distaste and she realised why. Her clothes were torn, obviously by the tree branches and they hung in tatters around her body, a human scarecrow.

It was as she entered this town that she realised in days to come that it was at the precise moment that she stepped foot in the town that her street days had begun.

A man was coming to the edge of town with a wheelbarrow of stale bread to dump it in the big dumpsite. Panaka's stomach gave a churn that seemed to connect with her legs and she found herself sprinting to fall on the bread before it touched the ground and with swift reptilian movements it was thrust into the mouth before the stomach could give its red warning light again, but it was not to be. The saliva needed for such swift endeavours had long since deserted the mouth leaving it nearly parched and the bread could not go to the stomach on its own accord, so it in fact lingered in the mouth stubbornly and the one that had reached the opening of the throat stuck there blocking the way.

The whole thing took less than a minute and Panaka's body responded by coughing out the bread that shot out of her mouth as if propelled from within by some inner spring and landed on the ground some metres away. Her body arched forward as bouts of coughs shook her spasmodic little frame, draining the remnants of energy from her body and the man was besides her, patting her back until she felt better and the coughing ceased.

She looked up speechless at the man. The unspoken gratitude was evident in her eyes and the man regarded her with gentle eyes. Her eyes were bloodshot as if she had just seen a ghost.

'You can do with some juice,' the man smiled, 'You are just the age of my own little girl. Come here I will give you a drink to go with the bread,' and the man took the wheelbarrow gesturing her to follow him.

Her teacher had told the class that there was a scourge of child trafficking and had warned the little children not to fall prey to these. In Panaka's mind, the words still rang clear as if they were an echo transcending time.

'I warn you all not to fall prey to these thieves for they are always after the heads of small children like you in order to get rich. They are very good-looking men or women with ever smiling faces who will entice you with nice gifts or tell you to follow them so that they will kill you. Never follow anyone you don't know or you will have your head cut...'

This statement decided for her, there was no way she was going with this nice looking man to get her head chopped off. With the swiftness of one who had been bred at the farms she snatched two loaves from the heap and sped away with a speed that surprised even the-would be Good Samaritan and left him shaking his head. *Just another street kid,* and he went on about his daily chores.

It was now midday, Panaka had found a spot halfway up a mountainside where she had sat and feasted on a whole loaf of bread and drank thirstily from a stream that flowed at the edge of the bottom of the mountain. After that, she had tried to formulate a plan on her next actions, but nothing could come through to her mind for she had not even a coin on her and the severity and futility of her situation assailed her with renewed vigour.

It was then that the first of life's lessons began to reveal itself to the young girl, that life in its wholeness was centred on the availability of money and that its absence, though live one may without it, but it rendered one paralysed and there would be no freedom of travel and manoeuvrability.

Money, it now occurred to her, was the centre of all activities. No wonder why people did all those repulsive things in search of it. She doubted that given her situation she could resist any evil to get it also.

At the farm, she remembered girls her age sleeping with men and doing vile things to secure money for small things such as sweets, to have their hair done and even so, they could have favours from the foremen at the farm during work. She had resisted all of the stuff back then, but doubted if she would this time around, given the predicaments she often found herself in during these last few days. In these last few days, her life had hit rock bottom. The abuses, the insults, the beatings all had been severe. She had slowly begun to doubt the existence of God, for how could it be possible that He would be up there and watch as she went through all that stuff and yet at the church, they said He was omnipresent?

It was also then that Panaka concluded that once the wheels of fortune stopped spinning in one's favour, then those of misfortune started spinning and the drums of doom took beat as if the one and only Creator had ceased to look after humanity. Panaka doubted that He could see her predicament now or if He was then He was ignoring her maybe for a reason and she racked her mind to try to find the reason in question.

Why would she be placed in such a situation?

She had heard that there was God from her teacher and from the Apostolic Sect that she attended on Sundays. A God who loved children and she was one of the children.

So why was He not showing the love now?

Was it because she was from the farms? Or did He have plans for her as it was said in the Bible verse her teacher taught them about? Was it a verse from somewhere in the book of Jeremiah or some other book?

But if her memory served well, the verse must have been in the book of Jeremiah chapter eleven.

Even as her mind moved round and round in circles trying to figure out ways out of her predicament, she felt her strength return as the hastily eaten bread did its work and she felt enlightened. *Where would she start to get money to go to Harare?* She decided then that she would have to beg for it. Beg on the streets.

Again, she realised that maybe not all of the children whom she found begging had no parents. Others may just be having parents at home, but would only not be satisfied by things at home and like her would be looking for money to execute plans which only God knew whether or not, they would see the light of day and if they did, whether or not they would rectify a life in jeopardy.

CHAPTER THREE

The thick blackness of night settled, bringing with it a very chill wind that blew across the land, punctuated here and there by drops of rain that were light and irritating. From the West came the rumble of thunder, deep and disconcerting like the roar of a male lion, which to the ear sounded the wacky alarm bells of warning about the coming of a rain to reckon with, the sound both frightening and irritating as if it were a warning of death.

The irritation wasn't lost on Panaka as she sat huddled in a corner in the big city of Mutare. Her hair was dishevelled and on her third day on the street, she could feel her bodily secrets being revealed.

Her body odours, the body being long since used to the art of being daily bathed, but having long since been denied such a privilege for days, began to nauseate even herself. She had never known that a body could smell so strongly and badly, like the smell of those very big male goats.

She was beginning to wish she had stayed at home with her mother and stepfather. At least she could be having a roof above her head and at least something in her stomach, no matter how little. But to her teenage mind, home was even worse than hell. It seemed to her that because of poverty, her parents were always at each other's throats and when they were not at each other's throats, then they were both baying for her blood. The fact that pained her most was that even at fifteen, a budding young woman, she did not even have a birth certificate, the lowest level of identification any citizen can have and her mother had used this as a way of reprimanding her each time she misbehaved, no matter how small the offence.

'*That's why I never get a birth certificate for you. You are a total disgrace to the family and me. You are just like your father, you smell,*' were words that she had heard nearly every day.

She had never seen her father and the only pictures she had of him were based on the snatches of history her mother told her about him.

***

Ronica was a form three student at a farm school, Helm Secondary School in the small farming town of Marondera. Her parents were farm labourers, working at a nearby farm, Forest Lodge Nursery where flowers were grown for export.

She learned with some richer students, children of farmers and landowners, young boys and girls who forgot that their parents' riches were not theirs and that for them to get their own riches they had to take school seriously and get good grades of their own in the quest to be like the parents.

These children went around school with their shoulders up competing for the best suitor and many admired them, these would be heirs of their parents' land. Little did they know that education was the only thing that one can boast of because it can never be stolen. It was such a calibre of students Ronica learned with and because she knew that her life was only defined by the confines of this compound, that both the inner and outer limits of her destiny was by virtue of her interaction with both the environment and the people in it she began to learn to accept the people as they were and to overlook the simple things that made them different.

In the farmlands, Ronica's life was simplified. She lived unpunctuated. Her routine did not vary, as did the events at the slow-paced farm school. Her life and the lives of the people around her seemed to advance through fixed gradations.

Few girls ever got to finish secondary school in these farmlands and it had become a norm. The cargo train of these girls' secondary education always slipped off the rails towards completion and no one batted an eyelid, the spirits of an area, which clung to even the most decent of girls. The life there was monotonous.

Things only got an abrupt start and the area's pulse began a fast pace with the appearance at the local school of a young male student teacher, Tonderai Sande. He was a thick muscled man of medium height with a neatly trimmed moustache. He had a bright liquid sparkle in each eye that made girls' fantasies dance on the far side of reason, a mass impersonator of all male attributes. He carried himself with grace of a martial arts fighter and girls at the school fought for his attention. Some girls wore mini uniforms and shreds of lipstick, but Tonderai did not spare a glance at any of them. He only laughed and shook his head at the ways of the farm girls.

One day whilst she was fetching water at the well a good distance from the farm compound, Ronica became aware of the presence of someone behind her. She spun around and her gasp of surprise was unconcealed when she saw Tonde the teacher smiling down at her from a height that seemed gigantic compared to her own dwarfed one which was hereditary, passed down to her by her mother.

'Why are you here? She asked stupidly. 'You must be in town at your house'.

'I have come for you, Ronica. I've loved you from the start,' came the reply.

Ronica couldn't believe her ears. *Did he want to play with her and desert her?* She had never been in love before and rejected all proposals that came her way. *Was this to be her undoing? Was he the heaven sent man? Was he to be part of her destiny?*

Her heart made a joyful leap in an unusual way as if it was telling her that this really was the man she was supposed to love. She couldn't believe it. Tonde the teacher?

He saw her hesitation and spoke softly to her. 'I'm for real Ronica. I have a hard time concentrating on teaching with you in class. You are all that I want in a girl. What I admire in you is your steady unwavering attitude to life, your resistance to withstand that peer pressure and mob psychology, that purposeful stance which makes you a cut above the majority of women in this world. You never tried to flirt with me like all the other girls. That's the kind of dignity I have been looking for. It's the law of life. A man selects his wife from the beautiful and humble minority that drifts in with the majority.'

It was socially unacceptable for a girl to admit love there and then, but then Ronica knew that it was not every day that a man like Tonde proposed to a girl like her. To her, it would be a rags to riches story, her own Prince Charming having sought her from the dusts of the farms. If she rebuked him, he might never come again.

What was she to do, agree? Wouldn't she be undignified for that?

Tonde solved the dilemma for her. He covered the distance between them in two great strides and took her in his powerful arms, his lips assaulting hers and smothering any reply that might have been on its way. She felt his hands on her body even as he crowded her backwards into some bushes. She had no control of what happened next.

Two days later, Tonde went back to college and two weeks later, she dropped out of school, pregnant.

Her parents couldn't accept this and chased her away. It was a mockery to the whole compound as Ronica was looked upon by most families as the only one who could outdo the spirit of the area, the spirit that saw to it that no girl completed school. She had become a role model to many and had let them down.

No one however discovered that this wasn't a spirit, that it was in fact something whose fault could not be placed on the children.

It was ignorance a lack of knowledge and the comfort of living in a world they had grown exposed to rather than explore the other worlds beyond and the pleasures and riches they provide, the world of education.

Ronica went to live with her aunt in Mutare farmlands where time brought about the birth of her daughter. She christened her Panaka after her own mother.

It was two weeks after the birth of her daughter that she heard the news that Tonde had gone abroad, deserted her. The pain was too much for her as she felt the trap of deception opening under her unwary feet.

**

'Hey, chick, what are you doing at the King's palace?' A voice brought Panaka back to the realities of the world and her current situation.

Her heart began a painful thumping against her tender chest. She had heard all sorts of stories concerning the street kids, *violent children of the streets, dwellers of plastic mansions that shook with the wind, kids of no mercy, the beasts of no nation,* people had termed them. For a fleeting second, her mind told her that she was now one of them, but her conscience was in strong conflict with this and she trusted it, for conscience they said in the church back at home was sometimes the silent voice of God.

'You don't have a tongue ha? You think that piece of meat between your teeth is there for design purposes? You say it's no tongue ha? I will give you one,' the boy loomed above her huddled form threateningly, a devil in a nightmare.

'I'm sorry. I just thought there wasn't …'

'Cut that shit bitch. No one doesn't know that it is forbidden to go uninvited to the King's palace. You think because we are on the streets the rules change?'

'Who's there at our place man?' Another high-pitched voice called from behind the first boy, then more voices until it sounded like a whole battalion of street children were crowded around her.

The voices were shrill and at that moment, Panaka did not recognise the voices for what they were, but looking back in days to come, she would know then what they were. They were the voices of adolescent boys high on drugs and with a brutality born of exposure to a world of extreme conditions long before their time, the voices of rage.

From the stolen glances she cast on them, she saw a group of children all dark in complexion as if they were born of one parent. They were all dirty and wore torn, battered clothing as if they were coming from a mine or they were the minerals being mined.

'Here's what you will get for that,' the boy said fumbling with the front of his trousers.

Panaka closed her eyes thinking that the boy was going to rape her for at home she had been led to believe that sex, drugs and food were the only things these street children were after. Then she was proved wrong. The boy was only unbuckling his trousers to release his thin leather belt that descended onto her back tactically cutting out a line that stung like hell's bees.

She screeched like an insane rat as she squirmed looking up and lifting her hands to protect herself. There were guffaws of unholy laughter from the group of urchins, and something again crossed her mind, a fragment from the past, memories of what people back at home said, that these children having long suffered on the streets, always try and find someone, a guinea pig to mete out their anger and with terrifying reality, she discovered she was at the receiving end of these boys' years of pent-up fury.

The boy lifted the belt again and Panaka closed her eyes, tensing her body, ready to receive the pain, but the blow never came. There was a sound, the sickening sound of bone making contact with flesh followed by a cry of agony. There was no mistaking the sound for her stepfather always beat her mother with clenched fists and the sound had become a part of her world. She opened her eyes.

Her assailant was holding the belt limply in his hand while the other caressed his jaw. There was terror in the boy's eyes, real naked terror. The nature of terror that must appear in the eyes of a buck in the face of a lion and even as she watched in suspended fear, the boy took to his heels and his fans quickly disappeared in different directions, wartime style as if the demons of hell were chasing after them with unholy fury. Panaka's eyes swivelled like a chameleon to the source of their terror. A huge bull of a boy stood looking at her from narrowed slits for eyes. The face was impassive, expressionless, the face of a person who had seen the worst in life and one more nasty experience could make no difference. His baldhead shone like a cannonball.

'Up and follow me girl,' the boy said. His voice was thick and gruff, a complete match to his thick manly features. She stood up quickly and followed on quivering feet, observing the boy from behind, studying him carefully.

He was dressed in tattered, filthy blue overalls that were several sizes smaller and which did little to cover his thick built manly features. The legs of the overalls were cut a little way above the knees barring his thick dirty hairy calves. The bulge of his warming blood vessels was distinctly outlined against a background of black hairy skin, ridges of hair high above the others worming their way all along the back of the leg.

His big feet were dirty with broken toenails and big cracks grinned at her from behind the feet in eternal mockery. They were forgotten neglected feet, feet that were as good as having been mined under a mixture of red and black soil, the resultant being a blend of colour now found on the feet of the street boy in front of Panaka.

'What is your name?' Came the gruff question.

The voice was very deep, a voice originating from deep within the boy where the hormones of manhood were probably at their highest.

'Panaka,' she said with a trembling voice.

'Where do you live?'

'I live nowhere.' She was near tears, her voice trembling and choking with emotion.

'I haven't seen you around here before,' the boy looked over his shoulder.

'I... I..., err happened to flee from home only six days ago,' she stammered.

'Why?'

And she explained.

'So you are going to be living around here?'

For an answer, she nodded behind him unable to formulate words to say to him, but he seemed to read her mind without looking at her.

'Then you need an ally. These streets are too dangerous for one to move around alone. The world out here is rough, the weather too is rough.'

'Where can I find one?'

'I am here,' the boy laughed. 'I'll be your ally.'

'Thank you,' Panaka felt a little relieved. 'Where do you sleep?' She asked gaining little confidence and relieved that he had offered to be her ally.

'We are almost there.'

'What's your name?'

'I am Alifu.'

'What a funny name. I've never heard of a name like that before,' she laughed nervously.

'I'm a Malawian.'

'Why are you here? I mean how did you come to live on the streets?'

'I was stubborn,' Alifu laughed. 'I didn't want anyone pushing me around. I just wanted to be my own boss.'

'Where did you live before you came here?'

'In Chikanga.'

'That must have been better than the farm where I grew up.'

'You will never know. They say never compare your life with others because you don't know what their journey is all about. Here we are,' Alifu stopped.

Panaka peered in the darkness. It was an opening to a dark alleyway. Alifu fumbled in his pocket and produced a piece of plastic with naked electrical wires dangling from it. He fumbled with it until some light emanated from it. It was then that Panaka discovered that what she had seen as plastic with dangling wires was indeed once a torch. She could safely say they were using the ghost of a torch.

'Follow closely behind me.'

For a moment, Panaka panicked. *Would she dare follow this boy alone into the dark?* If she didn't, where would she spend the night in such adverse weather?

'Are you coming?' Alifu asked from within.

'I'm coming,' she rejected her doubts. So far, the boy had helped her. She was now one of them so had to live their way and so she had to at least trust this one boy.

'Life on the streets isn't as tough as many may think,' Panaka said munching from a cob of boiled mealies.

Alifu shook his head. 'Life on the streets is very rough. It only loosens a little when one gets used to the streets.'

'Soon I'll get used to it, and then I'll try to learn to enjoy it.' Panaka shrugged.

'You are so eager to be a street kid?' Alifu laughed. 'Many of these children now wish they had a roof above their heads.'

'The streets look better to me than my stepmother's house. There is the promise of a sense of belonging, adventure and above all, an identity. I can go wherever I feel like going and I will visit places. Obviously I will clean myself up unlike them and always look presentable.'

'An identity as a gangster?' Alifu grinned.

'Don't talk like that Panaka. You just have to tell your father about all that is happening or even to try to go to live with a relative of your mother. The streets are not half as attractive as they seem in your mind. I once fled from home and lived on the streets, but only for the briefest of days before I went to find my relatives.'

In the dimness, Panaka saw blackness in Alifu's mouth. The boy had lost two teeth she realised, evidence of maybe some countless brawls in the boy's early teenage years. She shifted her gaze from the boy's face and her eyes went to the dark corner where some torn rags were heaped. It all seemed so well arranged, the boy's street schedule.

'How do you spend the day?' She asked.

'You're looking forward to it.'

'It's now my home it seems.'

'Then you'll discover for yourself,' Alifu chuckled.

'Do they all fear you?' Panaka asked recalling the scene back on the streets.

'Not much. I have been a street kid for ten years now since I was twelve. That means ten years' experience in street fighting whilst most of them are just one or two years old on the streets.'

'Why did you have to leave when you were still that young? You may have been just pushed by adolescent's doubt.'

'Do you really want to know what exactly happened?' He asked.

'Yes.'

'I'll tell you. There were other injustices in the past, but this was the last straw…'

'It was a particularly warm summer morning,' he began, 'and as expected I was sun basking with my two young twin sisters. My father's new Chaser was parked in the gate in front of the house. I lived with my father, stepmother and stepsisters. I was gripped by that adolescent urge to make conquests, went over my father's car, and peered in. There were no keys and so I went round into the house. On the doorway, I met my father and he greeted me warmly. You see my father loved me very much. Men rule the world, but surprisingly women rule men. It was my stepmom, I believe who injected into my father the seed of hatred, hatred for his own blood. As I got into the house, I met my stepmother and she scolded me for not doing the dishes first thing in the morning. As usual, I remained silent and continued on my way into the dining room. There in the cabinet drawer, I found the car keys, pocketed them and got on my way out. Again, I met my father on his way to the bathroom and he became suspicious for maybe guilt was written all over my face. "I can sense that you are about to embark on something suspiciously mischievous," he told me seriously. I only smiled and shook my head. I went back to the veranda and sat for some time, waiting for my father to start bathing. On the second thought, I went back into the house and returned the car keys. I couldn't take the risk. When I got outside, the girls were holding their mouths in fear and astonishment. I followed their gaze and to my horror noticed that the windscreen of the Chaser had cracked, the big crack grinning at us mockingly.

"Who did that?" Stepmom had come up behind me without me even noticing.

"Tasha threw a stone," Joyleen said.

"No it was you," Tasha spat back.

"No it wasn't any of you. It was Alifu,' my stepmom interjected. The twins looked thoughtfully at each other as the idea sank in, then at me and nodded. "Yes it was brother Alifu."

I spun around to face the woman in both horror and anger. "It wasn't me, I was in the house." I said.

"It was you. I saw you from the window and you ran into the house so that the blame will be placed on my daughters. I'm going to tell your father about this," and she turned on her heel and walked away. I panicked. What was I to do? It was clear that my father would listen to my stepmother's version as he always did. Even as I pondered about it, my father emerged from the house half-naked. He was fuming as he glared at the car, then at me. He pointed at the car. "How did that happen Alifu, tell me?" You should have seen the face,' Alifu laughed, 'that face showed no sign of humanity. Only a kind of solemnity that was more frightening than viciousness could have been. I couldn't look away from his face. I began to retreat, but he moved at a terrifying speed and yanked me by the collar. I began to scream my innocence, but they all fell on deaf ears. He dragged me into the bedroom, fished out an electric cord and whipped me whilst the door was locked from outside by my stepmom. When at last he stopped beating me, he was sweating all over and I could cry no more. I was too sore to move and he had to drag me to my room, dump me and locked me for four days with only breaks for recesses, I ate in the room. It was that massive beating and imprisonment that made me acquire a new slant on life. I couldn't help it and I came.'

Panaka knew by his faraway look that they were both seeing the past. 'I'm sorry about that,' she said, instinctively taking his calloused hand in hers, drawn by the urge to comfort that woman instinct, an inborn thing in every girl that make them better parents and that make them a man's greatest weakness.

'It's time to go home,' Alifu rose. 'You can do with some aid. It will help you relax dear.'

'What kind of aid?' Panaka was suspicious.

For an answer, Alifu took out a small plastic from a pocket in a short he wore beneath the pair of jeans.

'Hold out your hand.'

Panaka held out her hand and Alifu shook some white powder onto her palm.

'What is this?'

'This is the escape of the future. You sniff it and you will be okay. Use it especially when you looking for *echoes of the divine*,' Alifu chuckled.

'What do you mean by that?'

'It is the street way of saying when you're looking for oblivion. You see, it is one of the basics of survival I learned out there on the streets. There is no other way I could have survived those lonely nights, those very long nights in which even the dog feels lonely.'

'Drugs?'

'They are just a part of it. This is cocaine. I ran out of marijuana and some prefer glue, heroin.'

'If that is what you want,' Panaka sighed, 'then I'll take it, just for you. If it really makes you happy. I cannot deny you anything because you are all that matters to me now.'

'That's good,' Alifu beamed. 'Do exactly as I'm going to do.'

He closed one opening of his nose with a finger and drew

cocaine from his palm using the open nose. He closed the other opening and repeated the procedure. He watched Panaka do likewise and then laughed inwardly as he saw her react to the drug. Her voice began to slur and her vision blurred. She tried to fight her blurring vision to no avail and she surrendered to whatever world the drug was going to take her. She smiled as she was lifted up slowly into the air, defying the laws of gravity and was taken into space, dodging stars and going for the moon then fell asleep.

He arranged her into a comfortable sleeping position and cushioned her head. Then his eyes roamed all over her body the lust in the eyes barely concealed by the drugs in the blood.

He felt his own response at the sight of the opposite sexuality, but he knew the drug wasn't strong enough. He would wait and first earn her trust, and with these thoughts, he too drifted to sleep

It was a dark night and Panaka found herself on the edge of a very high cliff confronted by a ferocious looking dog that cut off her only means of escape. It was barking ferociously through a mouth whose teeth were not so good looking, teeth made primarily to bite through raw tissue and not to play around with tender stuff.

Step by step, it was approaching and step by step Panaka was retreating, losing ground until she stood on the very tip of the edge and looking down, she could see the world as only the gods would, from high up.

The objects below her were dwarfed and very tiny like the toys of Tiny City and there was that hazy bluish colour that accompanied any increase in distance, evidence that indeed it would be a long fall and neither would it be a fall to remember for by then her spirit and soul would have long since left a body whose identity could not be discerned by mere sight for it would have deformed on impact. *What was she to do?*

She turned back to face the dog, the bull terrier whose body bulged with muscle and flesh. Mastering her courage, she took a step towards the dog, threateningly, she saw it hesitate in mid-step, uncertain, and she took another step still. The terrier retreated several steps and Panaka, spotting an opening, made a dash for it and she ran, hearing the dog's breathing as it came after her.

She woke with a start, breathing heavily.

Her body was burning hot and she felt very weak. Sweat was coming out of her pores with a pace that was amazing and seemed inhuman. Her head felt heavy and hot and the air coming out of her nostrils was hot. In her mouth was a peculiar taste as if she had swallowed some Camphor cream and her muscles were tired and beaten up as if she had been in a fight with a boxer who had beaten her up on every available muscle of her tender frame.

The temperature began to drop rapidly until she was trembling and her teeth chattering. The fever of the near fatal dip in Nyamauru River had, like the long arm of the law, finally caught up with her and she found herself crying even as she lapsed into a deep slumber.

She did not feel anything as Alifu, having experienced lots and lots of cases of fever heaped pieces of clothing on top of her and took care of her as the fever grew. He watched her murmur incoherently as the fever reached its peak and racked her body until it subsided and her body returned to normal. The fever had passed.

CHAPTER FOUR

The heavy din of traffic and the noise and bustle of the city woke her. She looked around her, trying to gather her senses, surprised as to her whereabouts. Her eyes were wet with tears.

Her senses came and reality struck, hard and painful. Her hand went up to her face, wiping off the tears of long sleep and paving way to tears of another kind.

Her head felt groggy from the previous night fever, her limbs felt cramped, and she thought this was because of the drug. Alifu had risen early and was nowhere to be found. In the morning light, she scrutinised Alifu's lair. It was a square space in an alleyway that served as a drain. There was a heap of torn old blankets on one side and a heap of filthy old clothes on another. For the first time Panaka realised she hadn't been covered the whole night, but hadn't felt cold. It was the drug, she assumed. She hadn't had time for a blanket of any sort.

At another corner were dirty tins and cans, the boy's cooking utensils. They were spoiled with caked sadza. The place was dirty and filthy, but was better than the open spaces where she had slept the previous six days.

'I can see you are a late sleeper,' a voice said from behind.

Panaka started, spinning around, startled. She let out a sigh of relief. 'It's you, Alifu.'

'Yes,' the boy said, his lips moving trying to shape a smile. The result was a something more of a sneer.

In the morning light, the boy was worse looking than he had appeared to be the previous day. He was very dark in complexion, had small slit eyes and a big nose. His lips were big and sagged and when he talked, spittle escaped from in-between his lips.

'Are you going to stand there and stare the whole day?' Alifu's voice brought her back to reality.

'Oh, I'm sorry,' she blushed. 'How do you spend the day?'

'I should have eaten by now, but luck is not on my side today. I failed to get any food in the normal places. Well, let's go and see what we can get at Sakubva.'

Panaka let herself be led by Alifu, walking by his side, looking here and there into the rubbish bins and sometimes Alifu picked up an object of interest and laughed unashamedly as people watched.

Panaka kept looking around her, taking in the detail of the famous Mutare Township where she had never had the chance to visit, but had heard so much from her friends about. Cars and kombis sped by with a speed that was both fascinating and appalling.

Alone the past six days she had avoided the areas with lots of people, but now Alifu, dirty and dishevelled as he was, mingled with the people as if he was just another boy on a shopping spree.

'Who are those boys who keep looking at us and shrinking away?' Panaka asked. She had watched with growing concern as other street kids shrank away, regarding them with hostile eyes as they progressed towards downtown.

'They are the street children, our comrades.'

'So why do they regard us with hostility?'

'It's the way of the streets. Whenever a newcomer arrives, they'll be in for hell because an addition to the streets means greater competition for resources.'

'What resources?'

'The bins where the privileged throw away food,' Alifu

laughed. You will discover how important these things are during your stay in the streets.'

'But there are many bins in the town…'

'No, no, no,' Alifu laughed. 'There are many bins, but only a few are available. Some street bullies own certain areas and their bins. The other younger ones work for them. They do all the scavenging and surrender the proceeds to the masters who share the spoils among the servants. If you are caught scavenging unprotected in somebody's territory, then you will be brutally assaulted. Last year, one new boy was even murdered.'

'Murdered?' Panaka shuddered at the thought.

'Yes. There can be death on the streets and no one will raise an eyebrow.'

'Do you too work for someone?'

'Of course not. I told you I just want to be my own boss.'

'Then how do you defend yourself from the street tribes? Yesterday, about a whole battalion fled from you.'

'I am one of the bullies and I have servants of my own, never me working for someone.'

'So you must be tough,' Panaka was envious and the envy wasn't lost on Alifu.

'Do you think I would be sleeping in that good place if I weren't?' Alifu shook his head, 'No I wouldn't. It just pays to be tough on the streets.'

'Aren't you afraid of your servants turning against you?'

'A mutiny, a rebellion?'

Panaka nodded.

'I know some deadly martial arts skills for self-defence and I can surely pack a punch and sometimes you just beat them up to instil fear.' Alifu excitedly executed several martial arts moves in the full view of onlookers who looked on in awe at the skill he displayed.

Panaka paused, thinking then she asked. 'Are there any

other girls on the streets?'

She saw Alifu's features turn grim and his mood changed before he answered sourly. 'All the girls have been taken, abducted, stolen. I don't know what you may call it.'

'Abducted?' She was very alarmed.

'There is a certain tall and lean boy with cold blue eyes who works for some faceless rich man. He commands the gang and when they strike, they are dangerous. They raid the streets at night and take away street children, most of who will never be heard of again.'

'Oh, my goodness,' Panaka said touching her chest. 'When did they come?'

'It was not only once. In my ten years on the streets, they have come eight times. Each time we think they are gone for good, they strike again. It's a time of menace when they come. They never raid during the day because there will be too many witnesses around. If you resist, they whip you.'

'Why doesn't anyone report them to the police?'

'No one cares or seems to. The world is deaf of the cries of the forgotten children. We are the condemned and damned, identity less. We have scrawled several suggestions and thrown them into the suggestion boxes and the police come, not to protect us, but to abuse us. They are even worse than the raiders sometimes. At one time, a street girl was taken by the police and scrubbed clean before the males passed her around in their back room.'

'How heartless? When did the raiders last come?'

'Two years ago. It's the longest they've ever gone and we would like to believe they're gone for good, but everyone stays on the lookout.'

'What do they look like?'

'The boy leader is tall and lean with blue eyes. He is an expert at handling the whip and I'd like to believe…'

'Hey, Alifu, who is that bitch?' A boy challenged, standing

in their way.

Simba, the boy, was about Alifu's age, equally strong, but a little taller. His hands were thrust deep into the pockets of his tattered faded blue denim trousers. His chest was thrust out like a pigeon, a posture of arrogance and self-importance to an extent of being a challenge.

'That is none of your business,' Alifu spat.

Panaka realised they had passed a great many shops and were at the bus terminus a short distance away from the bustling activity of Sakubva Musika.

'It becomes my business when she sleeps anywhere she likes in my territory.'

'She did not sleep in anyone's territory. That was on no man's territory.'

'You threatened my boys when they told her. You now see yourself as King of the Streets. You forget your hierarchy Alifu, but I'll make you remember.'

'If you dare touch me –' Alifu hissed venomously.

Simba only smiled. 'I won't touch you, but they will,' he said pointing behind Alifu who turned to see five boys coming towards him. 'If you defeat them, only then will the Master interfere.'

Alifu faced the newcomers, instinctively attaining a fighting stance. The boys came to a stop and fanned out in front of him, grinning devilishly.

Panaka felt alarm welling up inside her. It was clear that Alifu stood little chance of winning against the boys. Her mind worked fast and she began to shout, 'Catch thief, catch thief,' she shouted pointing at Simba.

Simba was taken aback as passers-by came to a halt, as did most of the activity around them, looking at the dirty girl screaming. Then they looked at the even dirtier alleged thief and began to advance. The street King turned on his heel and ran. His five henchmen broke and fled in different directions.

Alifu walked up to Panaka, took her hand and left quickly. 'That was a bad thing to do.'

'Why?' Panaka was startled, 'I thought I was helping you.'

'It has created a grudge between our groups that may end in peril.'

'So were you going to defeat them?'

'These boys are from Sakubva and know as I do the secrets of Kung-Fu. They practice that every day. Let's go back. It's now dangerous to go to the Musika.'

'That's where they've gone?'

'No, but word will have gone there. They run the place and have syndicates around it. One may be killed in there and no one will say a word.'

They turned and went back the way they had come.

Heavy rainclouds hurried from the East to line up in the sky as if in answer to some divine summons. The wind howled like a hungry wolf roaring like a wounded tiger and assaulting the earth with terrific speed blowing sandstorms into the faces of the unfortunate few whose business was yet to be finished in town.

Panaka was one of those who looked at the gathering storm with dread. Had she been at the farms, she would have been happy to see the storms as it meant a break from continuous toiling in the fields.

'That's every street child's dread,' Alifu said looking up at the dark clouds, eating some snacks out of a plastic, which he had ravaged from the bins and shared with Panaka.

'How do you survive the storms?'

'In shop verandas, but we'll have nowhere to sleep.'

Panaka shook her head as she licked the dirty plastic that had contained the salted snacks. 'So what do you do?'

Alifu did not answer and she looked up. He was no longer looking at her. His eyes were somewhere else and she followed his gaze. Caught in the rushing crowd was an elderly man on crutches. He was counting money from a wallet and Alifu regarded him with open-eyed wonder. 'I'll be back in a minute,' he said and disappeared.

Panaka's eyes remained on the man as he pocketed his wallet and she saw Alifu appear beside the man. He deliberately bumped into him. The old man stumbled and Alifu helped him straighten up with apologies and disappeared. The old man continued on.

Alifu returned to Panaka, grinning from ear to ear, the old man's wallet in his hand.

'You took his wallet? You stole from a crippled old man?'

'He had some to spare,' Alifu said counting the cash and throwing away the wallet. 'We've earned enough for several days of massive feasting and we'll buy a fresh supply of glue and marijuana,' the boy was ecstatic.

'I'll not enjoy spending that ill-got money,' Panaka said bitterly.

Alifu regarded her seriously. 'This is the survival techniques of the streets, no courtesies or whatsoever. At least the old man still has a roof over his head and shoes on his feet and maybe love from friends and family unlike any of us,' the boy paused then went on grinning, 'We'll see if you don't enjoy spending the money, we'll see…'

**

Ronica sat cross-legged on the earthen veranda of her thatched kitchen in the farm compound. Her head was in her hands and her eyes were red from weeping. It was now a week since her daughter had fled and all attempts to find her were in vain. It was that maternal instinct of every parent who had endured nine months and undergone rigorous labour pains that made her weep now. *Why had her anger led her to scold her only daughter in such a way?*

How was she to seek the empty world again? She had dearly loved Tonde and Panaka was the last link between her and Tonde and was her only child having failed to bear her current husband any child. She was a monument to remind her of her first love, those special memories which no deed, no passage of time can severe, those wonderful emotions that bear testimony that indeed one is being ushered in a journey to the love station.

Her husband, the manager, was at work and she was wondering where her only daughter would shelter in the coming storm. The husband hadn't even showed any sign of loss by the fleeing of Panaka. His eyes had to her betrayed something close to relief.

That is when she realised that what people always said of single mothers when they got married again was true, that the maternal parent was always the best parent to the child and that if she ever let the child down, the only thing to expect from the stepparent was to do just twice that.

She discovered then that in her quest to please her husband, she had ignored the silent cries of her daughter, unspoken pleas that meant the world to Panaka and had created gulfs between mother and daughter, which would take time to bridge.

Every day scars were created in the heart of a daughter she had taken for granted and this she discovered is one of life's ironies. How life is a school whose lessons have to be lived in order to be learnt and how sometimes the damage cannot be undone.

Corrections in life's lessons it seemed were always left for the next generations. Young people whose knowledge of past shortfalls will make them appreciate even the smallest things of life.

*

The storm struck. It seemed as if an angry God had at last decided to break his promise to Noah and destroy mankind with water once again. As if he had just opened all the taps of heaven and some that had been reserved to cool-off hell if it overheated.

The rain came in torrents, falling at an angle in the whirling wind. Panaka and Alifu sat huddled in a corner of a veranda beside a fire of papers and boxes that smoked like a Cargo train, watching with bitterness as floods of surface run-off wove their way through the alleyway into their shelter. By the look of it, it would be days before the water level would fall and they would be able to use the shelter again.

'The floodgates of heaven have been opened,' Alifu said bitterly. 'Though it's to our disadvantage.'

Panaka was silent, thinking. She could feel bone-chilling shivers run down her spine even amidst the fire of boxes that cackled like a fool's laughter. The scene matched the death of her grandfather as narrated to her by her mother. Panaka's mind was about to revisit the events of that fateful day when Alifu broke her line of thought.

'Here, have this. It may help you get some sleep.'

She opened her hand and he shook some balls of marijuana into it. With experienced hands, she prepared the paper and wrapped the drug. Alifu lit it for her and she drew hungrily from the stub. She felt her head lightening, a heat wave swept across her whole being, and she marvelled at the wonders, which the drug always brought. Since her introduction to the world of drugs, she had not ceased to be amazed by the way drugs gave her comfort and a sense of well-being. To her, drugs were like good music giving peace to her mind and shortly shutting her from the outer world of mortal suffering. Her eyelids got heavy and dropped on their own accord and she fell asleep on the veranda.

Panaka woke with a start. Alifu sat by her side, ears cocked. There, from somewhere in the night, came the sound of raised voices, shouting voices.

'What's that?' She asked, alarmed.

'It must be a street fight,' Alifu said easily. 'They always occur in such weather.'

'Let us go and see.'

'I wouldn't advise that. It may be dangerous for you. Harmful weapons are always thrown and you may be caught in the crossfire. I'll go and check, if my boys are involved, they'll need my help.'

'Please don't take long, I'm frightened.'

'I'll not take long,' and he sneaked into the darkness.

After a few minutes, he was back.

'How bad was it?'

'As always, you'll see in the morning.'

'Why do they fight like that, in such a weather as you said?'

'Fights for shelter. Those who sleep in the open may feel compelled to raid those better sheltered. It will be time for survival of the fittest.'

Panaka shook her head. 'That's being uncivilised, barbaric.'

'Not anything like that,' Alifu shook his head. 'It's the way of the streets. It is the song of our life, all of it for our success as masters of the streets is measured by the number of fights we have won and by the comfort of base we have established to sleep.'

'I see,' Panaka said and see she did, for she realised that it was only when you had a descent roof above your head and enjoyed a mother's love that you consider the term *survival of the fittest* only in terms of animals. It had never occurred to her mind that even the human mind could be debased and degraded by the urge to survive. She had not imagined to what extent it could be lowered to a barbaric level in order to survive in a world where only the fit survived and like the animal world, the rest would be left to feed on the remnants of whatever the fit fed on.

Panaka cushioned her head in her hands, snuggled closer to Alifu and slept.

Again it came, the dream. The bull terrier was not giving up the chase, but instead was gaining fast upon her. She was in a forest now thick wooded, but there were many people and all were running away in different directions, each from an animal that was different from the next.

Some were running from snakes, dogs, baboons, but each was fleeing nevertheless and crying for help, not sparing a glance at the predicament of the next person. It occurred to her that each was in their own mind thinking that theirs was the worst.

The dog was fast gaining upon Panaka. She spun around and hauled herself desperately at the dog that, taken by surprise, retreated and stood metres away.

Again, she took to her heels, but her legs having fled for so long could no longer cooperate and she found them heavy, unwilling to comply with the weak mind. It was as if she were running through thick air and the effort sapped at the recesses of all her energy and she was breathing hard and gasping for breath like a pig that had choked on something even as an impenetrable brush appeared before her that cut off all escape routes and left her cornered.

It was then that she turned to face the dog, all the willpower to flee having dissipated under the cloud of tiredness and being replaced by another more sinister will, that urge to survive even against all odds. The terrier looked at her and snarled. She moved threateningly towards it waving her arms and it retreated some few steps and stopped, regarding the girl with wild yellowish eyes that seemed as if they were on fire. Summoning all the last of her strength and courage, she let out a loud scream and went for the dog, arms flailing wildly about her. The terrier could not believe this change of events and pinned its tail in-between its hind legs, gave a cry of anguish and sped off into the bushes. She woke with a start, her joy transcending the dream.

She woke up sweating and smiling that she had actually chased away that dog that had haunted her dreams. Her little mind had no way of knowing that this was in fact a revelation of some sort to her. That this was a lesson about the basic nature of the human mind, that a person always tend to flee from the troubles of life no matter how small they may be and that everyone regards their own problem as the worst and none spare a thought for the problem of others.

Another lesson which at this time eluded her young mind was that the human was just used to running away no matter how small the would be assailant may be, and that only when they have expended all available resources and exhausted all the other alternatives, do they get the ability to pull themselves and stand against their situations. Only then do they realise they lost themselves, their dignity and their time whilst fleeing from circumstances that were nothing, but chance encounters easily defeated and once defeated become nothing, but just memories.

But for now, nothing came through to Panaka and she took the dream as just one of those nightmares meant to strengthen a heart and it slipped her mind as she again drifted to sleep.

'This must have been one hell of a fight,' Panaka said as they wove their way among the crowd of shoppers who watched as municipality workers cleaned off the mess of the fight.

The brutality of it all was scarcely veiled by its simplicity. Drops of blood marked the road in a line as if to demarcate it. Jagged pieces of bottles littered the area a radius of about one hundred metres, as did broken sticks and stones.

It appeared as if men of a barbaric age long gone had been engaged in battle, the only difference being the absence of casualties on the scene. If there had been any, they had been removed from the scene in an act of comradeship that lived at the surface of the most barbaric of all civilisations.

'When they fight, they are like animals,' Alifu dropped his voice. 'Their anger being sated only by the sight of blood.'

'You can also be like that in anger?' Panaka asked looking into his eyes.

'I don't want to alarm you, but I can be more than that.'

Panaka felt her body shudder at the words. In his eyes were the glint of violence and she knew instantly that he meant it. Panaka hoped that she would never see Alifu in a fit of rage, let alone the anger being directed upon her.

CHAPTER FIVE

'You have learnt to live the way of the streets Panaka and all these must always be at your fingertips and you have to be able to execute these techniques and skills for you may never know when fate will part us ways,' Alifu was gazing unseeingly into space, the old man's money in his pocket.

'I think I've learnt already, Alifu. What else do you want to teach me? I now know the deadly skills of mixed Martial Arts and I now know how to surely pack a punch,' she said executing several moves from the JKD fighting style.

'There's one thing you haven't learnt to perfection.'

'That is?'

'The basic of street survival.'

Panaka frowned, puzzled and for an answer Alifu pointed at an old lady walking slowly with the aid of a stick. 'I want you to relieve her of whatever is in her pocket.'

'Oh, no, I can't. That's stealing,' she was terrified.

'That is one survival technique of the streets. You saw me do that several times didn't you? You even went on to enjoy the gains of the theft.'

'But I've never done that before, I'll be caught.'

'Once you have that fear of being caught, then you'll never get caught for you will act wisely. Now go.'

'I cannot.'

'I said go!' Alifu snapped, his eyes on fire.

Panaka stood up quickly, her eyes looking pleadingly at Alifu who ignored the look and went on. 'If you get caught you'll be beaten and if you don't get anything you will die of hunger. It is time you work for your food.'

Panaka   slowly   approached   the   old   woman   without confidence, her step carefully in check. Her heartbeat fiercely against her chest and she was breathing heavily. A lump came up to her throat threatening to choke her up and she swallowed heavily, painfully. 'How do you do grandma?'

The woman looked up and regarded the dirty young girl in tattered clothes with an air of suspicion. 'What do you want?'

'I-I-I-err saw you having difficulty and wanted to help.'

'Where do you live?' The old woman was arrogant.

'At the farms,' Panaka said moving closer to the old woman. She couldn't think of a better answer.

'Stay there,' the woman commanded. 'I don't like the way you look at me. You look like you can do with a bath too.'

But Panaka didn't listen. She moved closer, dipped her hand into the old woman's jersey pocket drawing out a wrapped cloth and quickly placed it into her underwear.

'Hey, thief!' The old woman shouted raising her stick in an effort to hit the girl. Panaka ducked her head and raced away. The woman lost her balance and fell onto the pavement crying. The cry was taken up and people gave chase after the street girl who had a good start on them. She ran as if all the legions of hell had been unleashed against her, making for the deserted areas of town cutting off chances of being intercepted.

Behind her people shouted, trying to stop her, but she was farm-bred and strong, long distance racing being her field of outstanding performance. She did the breathing technique, breathing deep in and out, breathing easy to keep premature exhaustion at bay. Slowly, the pursuing footsteps drew further and further away until they died off, but she kept on running deeper into the hills.

When convinced that she had outpaced them she stopped and sank to the ground panting and breathing heavily, her throat on fire.

'Caught you, thief!' A voice said from nowhere and Panaka scrambled to her feet, panic welling inside her. In front of her stood Alifu, breathing hard.

'You frightened me!' She sank back to the ground.

'I had to follow to protect you. You are very good Panaka. I didn't know you could run that fast.'

'I did athletics at school,' she said proudly in between gasps of air, which she greedily breathed in and out.

'Then you will be at an advantage in the streets. You'll unleash your talent here.'

'That was a close shave, Alifu. If people had caught me I'd have been dead.'

'What did you get?'

For an answer, Panaka fished out the cloth. It was a handkerchief and handed it to Alifu who eagerly unwrapped it and cursed disgustedly.

'What is it?' Panaka asked.

'It's only snuff wrapped around the cloth.'

'It is a bad thing I would have died for that.'

'It happens every first time. During my first time, I stole a wallet that contained only toilet paper,' Alifu grinned. 'But the second time you'll be lucky. This was just an introduction to the wonderful world of easy living on the streets. Now go and wait for me in those more secure hills. I'll go and get us something to eat.'

'I'll come with you.'

'No, it is now dangerous. You'll be recognised.'

Panaka nodded. She hadn't even thought of that. She discovered then that education and learning can be safely said to be two different things, for education is what is done in schools and learning is what is done in life, the accumulation of knowledge in different aspects of life and gaining experience in how to handle life's situations is learning and Panaka in effect did this in her street days. She learned.

She had in actual fact learned more there is to learn in life in her few days on the streets than in her days at home. She had been exposed to a world only a few ever get to know and her mind had outgrown her age. Unknowingly, she had mentally outgrown women twice her age and she would after all press on towards a destiny, which believers said was already pre-determined.

The sun was being buried on the distant hills drenching the Earth in a breath-taking orange gloom and lighting its grave with a dazzling spectrum of colour.

Even the stubborn white clouds embraced the beauty and took on the colour of the dying ball of fire knowing that it was to be short lived and marvelling with each moment they spent with the dying giant.

Alifu and Panaka sat on a stone in a mountain overlooking the Mutare Township and Dangamvura high-density suburbs. Both were chewing roasted mealies, which they had stolen from a nearby field and roasted over a fire they had built.

'Today we are going to sleep hungry,' Alifu thought aloud gazing unseeingly into space.

'Why?' Panaka's voice was muffled by the maize she was chewing.

'We've run out of our drug supply.'

'Oh, drugs,' she smiled. 'Where do you get them?'

'The dealers are now few and secretive. The police cracked down on them some months ago.'

'Oh, that's bad.'

'It's not as bad as you imagine it. It's worse than that.'

'Why?' She stopped chewing.

'It nearly cost my life,' tears welled up in the boy's eyes and he stopped chewing as memories assailed him and he stared into space.

Panaka was touched. 'How?' She reached out a hand and patted the boy.

'You want to know about it?'

'If you don't mind.'

'I'll tell you. I was the drug carrier,' he said, 'the boy who delivered drugs to their final destinations, keeping my eyes open and my services available at all times. I was trained to be a watchdog, on lookout for security men. It was nice. I was to connect drug addicts to suppliers and suppliers to some farmers. It was by pure genius and good police work that the security men cracked the drug ring and caught several suppliers and addicts in the act of trading. I had just left the rendezvous when they struck and was lucky to escape. This aroused the ire of the lucky suppliers who hadn't been present when the police struck. They hunted me down and snatched me from the streets in broad daylight. I was taken to a safe house somewhere in the low-density area of Fairbridge Park and they unleashed their wrath on me. They asked me questions, which I didn't know. First they pulled out my nails one by one using a pair of pincers.' Alifu spread out his hand for Panaka to see. She saw several nail-less fingers on his hands, something she had not noticed before. 'It was all so painful that I was reduced to a pleading and begging fool, uttering words that even to my ears had no meaning. They were words of pain, mumbled and indistinct. When they got no satisfactory answer, they changed the tactic and went for my teeth. They removed first the two front teeth using pliers this time. It was all so painful…' Alifu paused.

Panaka felt a faint cold chill as she imagined the pain Alifu must have gone through during those hours. All the time she had thought the boy lost his teeth in a fight.

'…you should have heard my cries. I was reduced to a sobbing, bleeding mess, the pain intense. It was by pure luck that the police arrived at that moment and the men tried to flee. All were apprehended and I was sent to a hospital where I learned that the police had acted from an anonymous tip-off. I fled from the hospital after four days and went straight to raid one of the drug safes in the mountains. I didn't sell them and became an addict myself. I am now afraid of suffering from after effects if I try to stop. So it was after that incident that I became reckless about life, after all mine wasn't even worth all that trouble.'

'Don't worry, Alifu,' Panaka said soothingly. Her heart had been touched by his story. 'One day things will be okay and you'll live everyday like a holiday. You know, I dream that one day I will be a mother and have lots and lots of children with a loving husband, most probably a banker or an accountant who returns home to kiss me every day. I will give extra care to my children,' she hugged herself as she was lost in her fantasy whilst Alifu looked at her as she went on. 'You know, I want to have around five children a car and own a very big home with lots of relatives and friends around.'

'And how do you plan to achieve that,' Alifu asked.

'Don't tell me you are content to live in the world you have found yourself in Alifu. It really is not yours. It may be in fact a transit phase in life, a very low step with light at the near end, a period of darkness which may be intended to make you appreciate light in the coming future. Let not this life leave you beaten Alifu. There is always light at the end of the tunnel. Just pray and believe in God.'

'Don't tell me you can even have hope in such a situation. There indeed is no hope left in this life or even in the life after, if there is even anything like that in the world.'

'Yes there is life after death and the Bible proves that. It tells of a world beyond this world, a life to come. You have to hope for a greater and much better life and living in the suburbs won't be out of the question.'

'I don't think so. I have been growing more irritable with

the passage of time and a flashy home may be worse than the streets.'

'Why?' Panaka frowned. 'It is every street child's dream, a big home with a tall fence or brick durawall, a nice flashy car and a happy beautiful wife.'

Alifu shook his head grinning stubbornly. 'It would feel lonesome without this gangster element I have become used to. I have become used to ordering my boys around. Maybe if I become a politician or a military Commander, only then will I be content to leave the streets or else I become Master of the Streets.'

'You fool,' Panaka punched him playfully and they both laughed.

'It's growing dark, let's go,' Alifu said standing up and offering his hand to Panaka who took it and went towards town.

'I'm going through Sakubva to try and secure something for the night. Go straight to our place and I'll be there soon.'

'Don't take long,' Panaka said. She still feared to walk the streets alone.

'I will be there soon…' and he began to jog.

Left alone, Panaka realised that many times in life first impressions can be deceiving yet a lot of people claim the *first cut is the deepest* and that the first impression always lasts the longest.

Her first impression about Alifu, she realised, was nothing near his actual personality. The boy that the streets had made of him was nothing compared to the boy he was within. She had thought he had lost his teeth in a fight yet it was something more sinister than that, a situation beyond his own liking.

Again, she had taken him to have a bullish character yet she had discovered a soft spot in him, a part that was the boy within, overshadowed sometimes by the boy the streets had made out of him. She discovered that beneath the veneer of his martial arts skills that made him bullish, beneath the hardened and beaten up boy that the streets had made of him, the boy had a spot in his heart which if correctly triggered would make him fit in the society from which he had been estranged for so long a time.

This is the nature of the human being, to always adapt to whatever situation and environment he is exposed to, but there is always that place deep within from which his real personality always thrives.

CHAPTER SIX

Darkness had descended faster than Panaka imagined it would. She made her way towards her aunt's home, lost in a pool of memory. She thought of her mother back at the farms and all the days she had spent there as she grew. She realised how she had thought hers as being the worst condition in life back then.

She hadn't even thought that there were other children out there who never even had a proper shelter, who had no parent to plan their meals and who faced each dawn with dread.

She had back then thought that living with a stepfather was a plight unmatched in the history of civilisation, unknowingly that some children never even saw the face of a single parent and they longed to live even with the worst of all stepparents as long as they at least had somewhere to lay their heads and a stomach even though not full, but at least with something in it other than the winds of a thousand pained breaths of the streets.

It is a wonder how most people in this life take their fate as the worst in life no matter how petty it may be, how even losing some little cash to thieves may lead people to say it is the worst that can happen in life.

Most never think of some others who lost everything they would ever have, few think of the little children roaming the streets who lost their lives before they even got started, people who ceased to live the moment they were born, but only to exist in a state of nothingness in which they may become citizens for the rest of their days. Few, very few ever came near a plight as this and only a fraction even among those who had grown to white hairs came near to experiencing such a fate, a life of the forgotten.

Thieves, many say these children are, but it was only now that joy, after befriending one of them began to realise that it was not their nature, but instead the horrors and conditions to which they are exposed to mould them into characters they never were and snuff out some recessive personalities that exist on the periphery of their humanity coming into being only when the balance between civilisation and barbarism topples over.

No one seemed to spare a glance at the dirty citizens of the streets or if they did, then their ignorance was like the characters of a movie, convincing and well executed.

She was whisked out of her reverie when she heard footsteps behind her and she turned, an instinct city life had painfully grilled into her as her aunt instructed to her some of the basics of living in the city.

A grinning face belonging to a thickset boy loomed into view. Panaka's heart made a terrifying lurch and began to beat heavily.

'I've got two dollars and need some time with you,' the boy said. It was clear from his dressing that he was a boy of the streets. She had quickly come to know exactly how to discern the children of the streets from the children on the streets.

'No, I'm not interested. Go away.'

The boy seemed unmoved by the response. 'Then I'll take you for free.'

'No,' Panaka said firmly attaining a right lead fighting stance, one of those she had been taught in her self-defence lessons her aunt paid for her, as the boy stretched out his hands walking towards her.

'If you dare,' the boy snarled and fished out a long bladed

knife grinning devilishly. 'I always get what I want. Besides, the streets are no place for Virgin Mary and you cannot refuse me anything.'

Panaka felt panic welling up in her chest as a wall came up behind her. She was trapped. Her eyes darted sideways, looking for an escape route. She saw the evil gleam in the eyes of the boy as be brought his face to within inches of hers and she could smell his stale breath coming in gasps that indicated his excitement. It was clear that if she screamed, the boy would stab her and run. Aunty had told her many such cases.

'I'll have you here, right here,' the boy said as he fought to unbuckle the front of his canvas trousers, which looked more like regulation prison garb.

'No, you'll not have her,' a voice said from behind.

The boy spun around, but it was a mistake. A strong hand shot out and seized his neck as another chopped his wrist, disposing it of the knife that fell down with a clatter. Alifu held the boy's neck in a deathly vice with fingers like a steel trap.

Panaka saw a liquid flood soak through the front of the boy's trousers as his bladder emptied in naked terror. The boy's eyes bulged out as his mouth moved, trying to form words. What came out were choked sounds that were like a cat with a ball of wool stuck in its throat.

'Go, Panaka, I'll teach this fool to revise his manners,' Alifu said, and Panaka saw a glint in Alifu's eyes, something she had not seen before.

There in his eyes was a madness, the glint in the eyes of a lion before a kill, the glint in the eyes of a snake before it strikes, it was the unmistakable killing madness and Alifu's voice cut off any compromise and Panaka like a rat freed from a steel trap scurried off into the night.

When Alifu arrived at their shelter several hours later, he

was carrying a plastic full of fruits and smiling. 'They always pay tribute if they do me wrong.'

Panaka saw the caked blood on Alifu's knuckles and instantly knew that he had somehow forced out the tribute.

'What would you have done had I not come there in time?'Alifu asked.

'I don't know,' Panaka replied truthfully.

The question had not occurred to her what she might have done. She doubted that she would have given a fight in the face of such an evil looking knife and doubted that she would have been able to execute the few martial arts moves Alifu had taught her. According to her teacher at school, it was only God who had sent Alifu at that precise moment to spare Panaka the pain of bearing this shame for the bigger part of her life. *If it was God*, she thought, *then to him be the glory.*

CHAPTER SEVEN

'We have a new girl in our group,' Alifu addressed his group of followers as dusk approached. 'Her name is Panaka and let's all welcome her.'

'Welcome, Panaka,' the group chorused clapping, but their faces did not show any sign of welcome. A member meant less shares, especially a girl.

They knew they had a duty to feed and protect her and Alifu would take her all by himself, but they couldn't voice their opinion. They knew their leader well. He did not want to be angered. The boys from the group walked away in clusters leaving Alifu sitting with Panaka in the park eating pies, a rare meal especially in their world.

Alifu had in fact snatched the pies from the hands of an unsuspecting teen couple who had been making their way towards a secluded part of town, probably to make up, but had abandoned the idea when they parted ways with their pies and had given no chase after the dirty boy of the streets.

'What a touching scene.'

Alifu and Panaka both spun around to see Simba, the self-acclaimed King of the Streets and several of his followers standing behind them. Instinctively, he whistled and his own dispersing comrades ran and took position behind him.

'We don't want to start one hell of a street fight like we did several days ago to those bastards who didn't want to give up their shelter in the rain and we severely punished them,' the King said opening his shredded jacket to reveal the knife in his waistband. 'I have come to give you a nudge, a warning you may say, to keep to your territory.'

'I've heard that before.'

'I told you I'm not here to start a war,' the King looked behind at his followers who took out knives and brandished them. 'For we are over prepared for that.'

'If it's a war of knives,' one of Alifu's followers stepped forward. 'Then we all did our homework.'

He lifted his T-shirt to reveal a dirty shrunken belly button and fished out a long bladed hunting knife from the waistband of his boxer shorts.

A flicker of doubt passed over the King's face but he smiled wickedly. 'You seem to be out numbered in weapons.'

'Are we?' Alifu's follower asked turning to his friends. There was a chorused. 'No!' And knives were fished out, bigger than the ones belonging to the King and his friends.

'No!' Alifu shouted. 'We don't want an unfair knife fight. If the King of the Streets wants to settle a score, then let it be one on one stand.'

There were chorused acknowledgements from both groups and another from a gathering third group.

There was a flicker of doubt across the King's face who had never been challenged before. Darkness was falling and there was no doubt whose side the third party would take if things turned for the worst. Simba knew that the third group were definitely not his fans.

'There is not enough light for a decent fight. If that indeed is a challenge, then we'll meet tomorrow at daylight.'

'No, coward, you want to run away. You'll fight in the torchlight,' someone shouted and torches were fished out, the crowd fanning out to create a ring for the fighters.

The King took off his jacket and handed the knife to one of his followers.

Alifu took out a knife Panaka had never thought existed and handed it to her. 'No, don't fight please, Alifu!' She tried to pull him, but he pushed her away. His strength was terrifying.

'I'll be the referee,' the leader of the third party came forward between the two with a stick. 'No one will cheat. Here we go,' and he stepped aside.

The two fighters were all professionals. They did not jump for each other, for each knew what was to be done. This was to be a systematic fight. They both attained the right lead fighting stance and circled each other warily, trying to spot an opening, Simba bouncing up and down on the balls of his feet building up on confidence.

The group of followers shouted the names of their own, urging them on. The King loosed an arrow punch. Alifu sensed rather than saw the punch and ducked, feeling the fist grazing his right ear and the power behind it wasn't lost on him as his ear went hot. Even as he marvelled at the punch, Simba came at him with a straight kick in the groin and he felt his world burst into a shower of sparks as he stumbled backwards, but kept his balance, circling and waiting for his vision to clear.

Sensing his advantage, the King went for him with a double fist punch, which Alifu countered with a double block and loosed a powerful stopping kick that caught Simba in the groin and he shrieked. That was the mistake.

Alifu knew the boy had been hurt and he executed a deadly in step that he coupled with a back-fist to the nose and he felt something warm and sticky wet on his hands, red in the torchlight even as Simba staggered like a drunken hobo, his face contorted with pain, anger and disbelief. He regained his balance and attained a boxer's stance that drew cheers of encouragement from his group of followers whose loyalty to him had reached the levels of near worship to the self-proclaimed King of the Streets for he seemed to know a lot about life having been better educated before he came to the streets.

The King went for Alifu with the fury of a wounded

animal, executing a dozen karate chops, fists and jabs ready to chop and punch whatever was in his way. One of the punches caught Alifu on the mouth, he tasted blood and staggered backwards, off balance, and Simba moved in for the kill, grinning murderously in the mystic torchlight, devilishly.

There was a shout from the crowd and suddenly everyone was running in different directions shouting and cursing.

Alifu ran and took Panaka's hand and joined the fleeing crowd. For a moment, all opposition was forgotten as the street children fled, most of them in the same direction.

'What is it?' Panaka asked as they came to a stop several blocks away out of breath.

'It is the police. They'll catch and beat you out of your skin.'

'So what about the unfinished fight?'

'I think it's already finished. The King has never been challenged before. He always exercised his strength by beating without any challenge or resistance. I have always been dreaming about his downfall.'

'So you've won?'

'Not yet, but by now I am being regarded as the new King, a title which someone else may claim from me overnight.'

'Hey, you, stop there!' A voice commanded.

Both turned and saw a policeman before they took to their heels into the night, easily outpacing the lone officer.

CHAPTER EIGHT

Three Months Later

Panaka tightly clamped her jaws and lips as she rushed out of the shelter into the darkness of the night feeling all her muscles tense as a feeling of nausea swept through her. She crouched several metres away and retched.

She had been feeling this nausea for two weeks now and sometimes it was coupled with dizziness. She had told Alifu about it and he had laughed it off as a change of diet from the warm clean meals of home to the little spaced meals of the streets.

'You were serious about your pregnancy fears.' She had not heard Alifu as he came to stand behind her.

'Pregnancy?' She sounded alarmed.

'Yes, that's what it is. Street pregnancy.'

'How do you know?'

'I've heard about all the symptoms from experienced women.'

'So what do we have to do?'

'The only way to deal with unwanted pregnancy is to terminate it.'

'Abortion, no, I can't do it!'

'There's no other way. You barely have enough to eat, what more to give and feed another helpless mouth.'

Panaka began to sob.

'Stand up now, let us go to see an expert to take care of it.'

'I don't want to go, Alifu. I'm not going,' she shrugged him off.

'That's nonsense. We're going.'

'I'll call for help,' Panaka threatened. She had heard many stories about botched abortions with both the mother and foetus dying in the ditches unattended.

'If you cannot do it, then you'll have to find your way about the streets. I'm washing my hands out of this.'

'But you are the father.'

'Then if the father gives a command and you disobey, he can be justified if he walks out of your life like I'm doing now,' he turned and began to walk away hands thrust into the pockets.

'Alifu, Alifu!' She called hysterically

'Yes.'

'I'll go.'

The room was confined with pieces of old furniture, which were dusty and neglected. The old woman sat on a chair across the table from Panaka and Alifu. The air in the room was choking and fetid, smelling of stale tobacco smoke and sweat and Panaka wondered how many other girls had sat in those chairs across the woman frightened as she were now.

It was then she discovered that fear was something that had no extent and there was no limit to the extent of fear one could experience each day as an individual. First, she had experienced fear of her mother as a child, fear of her stepfather and she had in those days seen these as the two greatest fears. On the streets she had been exposed to a whole lot different type of fear, fear of starvation and fear of being caught in a street fight. Nothing had however prepared her for the fear now enveloping her whole being. It was the fear of death, a fear so strong nothing could stand firm in its way and nothing in the history of humanity could defeat its clutches or deceive it.

'Are you ready to carry the risk?' The woman asked.

Panaka paused, looking for words. Alifu nudged her from under the table and she answered. 'Oh, yes, yes.'

The woman regarded her doubtfully in the dim light. 'I don't want an army of police officers coming here looking for me.'

'She's okay with it,' Alifu said.

'Right,' the old woman said. 'Since you have paid you can leave her with me and you'll come for her tomorrow. You will know what to do after collecting her.

'I'll just wait for her and…'

'You are no longer trusting me err?'

'No, okay I'll come for her,' Alifu said reluctantly. He did not want the idea of leaving Panaka behind with the old woman for the whole night. The old woman was full of tricks.

He stood up, took Panaka's hand in his and squeezed her reassuringly before he left.

The old woman waited for ten minutes after Alifu had left and beckoned the girl to come closer. She saw the girl hesitate before she snarled at her. 'Are you afraid of me?'

'Certainly not.'

'Then follow me into the operating room,' the old woman stood up and went into one of the bedrooms with Panaka following behind.

In the bedroom was a comfortable three quarter bed and Panaka was told to lie in it and she complied.

The old woman took out a bottle containing a strange concoction, opened it, poured some into a cup, and offered it to Panaka.

'It is the escape from pain, powerful and exhilarating. You will have a strange sense of flying through space. You have to take it in one gulp for maximum effect and it will help you relax.'

Panaka closed her eyes and took the liquid as

commanded. She felt her muscles relaxing and her head lightening even as her head dropped and she fell into oblivion as the old woman laughed.

The young girl wasn't aware of the four men who entered the room on the old woman's summons. She did not even feel a thing as she unknowingly used her body as a sexual weapon as men paid the old woman to sate their lust on the unfeeling young girl. It was after several men had sated themselves that the woman carried out her operation and she was several dollars richer.

When Panaka woke up in the morning, she felt as if she were floating in an endless ocean of pain. The pain was all over her body seeming to spread from head to toe. She groaned as she lifted her head. Her eyes felt groggy and hesitant to open and when her vision cleared she realised she were soaked in blood, her own blood. Her head dropped back onto the pillow and she moaned.

She heard the door open as if in another land far removed from the one she existed in and Alifu's face appeared in her line of vision. She tried to talk, but only incoherent sounds of pain escaped her lips.

When he saw this, Alifu instantly knew what she did not know. He had trusted the woman and now his fears were confirmed. The girl had been gang raped. He clenched his fists and grit his teeth together as he looked through the window. He couldn't take Panaka out in that condition in broad daylight. He was going to wait until dark and carry her away before meting out vengeance on the old woman.

He knew exactly that he could not touch the woman because she was always surrounded by her stout looking young men who were her security men.

Again, he could not go to the police for first they would ask for his identity before anything else. Who would like to listen to the story of this dirty young man? Above all, abortion was a crime that would see him and Panaka put in jail.

For now, there was nothing he could do. He decided retribution in this case was going to be left to the one whose identity could not be questioned, one whom everyone spoke of, but none had seen. Vengeance in this case Alifu decided was going to be left to the Supreme Being on whose decision no human can dispute. Whose name was always talked about in public, the Creator of the human race whose timeless vengeance on the cruel was always well-defined and unquestioned.

Vengeance, Alifu decided, was not for the mortals. One day an angry God will fall down to earth to mete out justice onto the unjust and maybe then Alifu hoped, the old woman would be among the unjust.

CHAPTER NINE

Time flew and Panaka grew accustomed to the ways of the streets. Her hair grew long as did her fingernails and Alifu occasionally cut them off. She became accustomed to drugs and sex on the streets. She had sex with Alifu in their lair and sometimes hooked up clients at popular nightspots. She learnt how to steal from people's pockets undetected, how to con people and how to protect herself on the streets.

She had become a mistress of the streets and now had many friends. On the streets, she discovered the children had forged a community of its own, well organised and run where everyone had his own peculiar identity and all knew what was to be done. Days flew uneventful until one night when her temporary peace was shattered.

It was a particularly dark night when Alifu crept into the lair breathing hard. His eyes were wide open with an emotion, which she quickly deduced to be fear. They were filled with such naked terror that she panicked. Never had she seen such naked terror in eyes of man.

'What is it, Alifu?' She asked holding him.

'They are here – we've got to go.'

'Who?'

'The Men of the Whips.'

'Which men, the kidnappers?'

'Yes, they've already raided the other side of town.'

'So what must we...'

'Shhh,' he placed a finger on her lips and paused, listening.

The heavy din of running footsteps wasn't lost on them. There was a sharp crack and someone screamed.

'It's the whip, oh my God!' Alifu moaned. 'Let's run for it!' He pulled Panaka and crawled outside.

She followed behind him and reached the opening. It was cold and dark outside. Alifu let go of her hand, motioned her to follow and made a dash into the darkness. Panaka clumsily stood up to follow, but fell back onto the ground as a sharp crack pieced the night's air to her right and a voice bellowed. Her heart made a quantum leap as she felt and tasted the cold, chill sensation of fear.

She couldn't stay where she was again. She had to go. She scrambled to her feet and made a dash in the opposite direction towards the lighted shop veranda, glancing back to see if she was being pursued. Swifter street boys overtook her, the legends of the street who rather glided as if their feet where not even there, ignoring her cries for help.

She suddenly stopped in her tracks.

A dark figure was silhouetted in her way against a lighted background. She clapped a hand over her mouth as she saw something dangling at the figure's side, a whip. She began to retreat slowly as if she were invisible.

She greatly wished that some divine power would descend from the heavens and take her in a puff of smoke to Nirvana, the land of bliss that is barren and clean, free of pestilence.

'Don't try to make a run for it girl,' the voice cut off her thoughts. 'I don't harm ladies,' the voice was soft and coaxing. 'We are here to give a new life to the homeless. Come to me and I promise that no harm will befall you.'

Panaka stood looking at the figure, weighing the truthfulness of those words. Her eyes held the figure, which seemed to emanate power to give a bright future, but then the devil, her mother had once told her, came like this, soft spoken and gentle yet with a heart that was as spoiled as the acts to which he was up to. The man took a step towards her.

'No, murderers!' Panaka spun around to make a dash for it, but she flew straight into a pair of outstretched arms. 'Leave me, leave me alone!' She began struggling.

The man held her with an iron grip and she felt a needle pierce her arm before hitting a vein. The fighting power fled out of her as darkness engulfed her. A distant voice spoke to her in the blanket of darkness. 'Tonight is the night all your frustrations end and we've got a really nice surprise for you.'

She blinked her eyes, tears of blunt hurt filling them, disorienting her but somehow providing a measure of relief. Her mouth was filled with the dried spit, which accompanied any lengthy period of breathing in pain. She lifted her head to examine her surroundings.

She was in a clean smelling room, the fragrance of flowers so intimate and overpowering after the overwhelming street smells, that she wanted to cry. She lay on a bed that was soft and comfortable.

As if in a haze, she slowly climbed off the bed and walked around the room, a girl walking in a dream through a land both fascinating and frightening as if in a dream.

Why was she here? Why was she alone? Where were her captors? Nothing seemed to make sense. The room was well equipped as if it had been made for a model in a beauty contest. If she were to be killed as Alifu had said, then why all the courtesy? *Why all this luxury? Was there any reason to do this to a prize ready for slaughter?*

She caught her image on the wardrobe mirror and gasped. She did not remember herself looking like this. A transformation had occurred. She was clean looking and her hair had been cut and shaped neatly. Instead of her filthy street clothes, she was now in a flimsy nightdress reaching just above her knees. She was transformed from a street girl to a beautiful looking prisoner.

'I can see you are already enjoying the luxuries our organisation has to offer or might I say some of the minor ones,' a voice said from behind her.

Panaka spun around, surprised. Somehow, the door had been opened and the man had walked up to only a few steps of her, his movements muffled by the carpet.

He was clean shaved and not evil looking, as she knew kidnappers to be. He had boyish features, tall and lean with blue eyes.

The eyes struck her and she remembered Alifu's words, "*the boy has cold blue eyes*,", but the eyes were not cold now. They were warm with amusement. He was staring, she realised, not at her face, but on her chest area. She folded her hands across her chest and shrank back, frightened of what his intentions were.

'Don't worry, I'm not going to harm you. We could have done that when we captured you. I've just come to take you to see the boss,' the boy laughed.

'The boss? You are not going to…?' Panaka couldn't finish the sentence.

'Kill you?' he finished for her. 'No, it is what your street comrades think. You will find out otherwise. Get dressed. There is a blue dress in the wardrobe. I'll be waiting outside,' and the man strode out, closing the door behind him.

Panaka walked over to the wardrobe and paused. *What did she have to do? Obey?* It seemed the only sensible thing to do now.

'She is quite a sexy little thing,' the middle-aged man said puffing out cigarette smoke. The high ridges of his cheekbones could have been sculptured by an angry artist.

'She is an attractive and naturally beautiful girl, with the figure of a hometown beauty queen and physically equipped to be a film actress.'

Panaka listened to this as she stood before the man who was flanked on either side by uniformed guards. She felt like a prize stallion as the man passed his comments, examining her like a horse for sale. She had recognised the man the instant she had seen him. He couldn't be missed by anyone. He was a Minister cum businessman whose face appeared on television very often doing charity work and donating to the needy. He was one of the lucky beneficiaries of the diamond industry, a man who now was only being referred to as Kedha.

'I understand you have been briefed on your job description,' it was a statement.

Panaka nodded, emotion chocking her and making it impossible for her to speak.

'And from what I take you've liked it?'

Panaka again nodded. She had been using drugs on the streets and the prospect of working again with drugs fascinated her though this time it would be on a grand scale.

'Now, before we heard your story last night…'

'Last night?' Panaka was startled. She did not remember ever talking to anyone after the injection upon her capture.

Kedha let out an easy laugh. 'Yes, last night while you were being bathed. Believe it young lady, this is the age of drugs. Your mouth did the talking, but your mind wasn't in full control. You are Panaka, identity-less and a street kid for about eight or so months.'

'I see, you are right,' Panaka said. She was beginning to discover that cooperation was the only thing she could do in order to lessen the weight of her fate, besides she had come to realise these people were not going to harm her in any way, but were instead offering her a job and an identity.

'You can take a seat,' the man said and she gratefully took one. Kedha dismissed his men with a slight wave of his hand and the men scurried out of the room. Left alone, the man's eyes roamed her body for a full minute. She was feeling uneasy when the man broke the silence.

'I gathered that from your job description one important aspect has been left out,' he paused.

Panaka said nothing. She just looked plaintively at him.

'It's a nice thing you agreed to the job even before this thing was introduced, so it'll be a welcome addition I presume,' the man paused and relit his cigarette never taking his eyes off the girl.

He admired her. After spending time on the streets, her face was systematically void of expression such that whatever went on behind the smokescreen of her eyes, nothing came through to him.

She isn't fit to be a farm girl, he thought, *but if she claims as she did that she is, then she is a cut above the rest.*

'The addition is when you'll be our drug courier as explained earlier. I also want you to run for me one of my *houses of comfort.*'

'What is that?'

'A whorehouse stripped of its verbal frills, that's what it is.'

Panaka could have been shocked, but she wasn't, not after the nights she spent with Alifu, with Alifu teaching her things about her body that she had never thought existed. He had taught her to play games with her body and had confided with her how she could use her body to feed herself.

She had even laughed at one time when she heard how at one time Alifu had tried to use his body to feed himself, but gave up when one day after the act.

When Alifu had told her all this, it was as if time had no meaning.

'Are you considering the offer?' Kedha's words brought her back to reality.

'Where are the others you kidnapped the night you took me from the streets?'

'They're going somewhere very far away,' Kedha laughed. 'Somewhere you'll never see them again and I knew you'll not like it where the others are going, that's why I spared you the journey.'

'Where are they?'

'You don't want to join them, do you?' Kedha was suddenly serious.

Panaka thought quickly and shook her head.

'Right, then stop asking. I've got a very healthy temper,' the man smiled disarmingly.

It seemed to her that Kedha had come out of the blue for a date destiny had scheduled long ago. It seemed that all her years had been vying for this. This was to be her destiny. From the start, her life had always been scheduled to culminate into this.

'I'll take it,' Panaka didn't hesitate. Sex without love wasn't always my dream, but I'm always prepared to drink from life's proffered bowl.'

Kedha smiled triumphantly. 'You are a clever lady. You will have all the luxuries of life so you will discover that you will willingly do without the necessities. The pay will be handsome. You will have tight protection and security around you and above all, you will have an identity, a new identity in a world where you have a sense of belonging. Old days and old ways must be swept away to make way for the new,' he offered his hand, standing up.

'Thank you, sir,' Panaka shook his hand and stood up. She was startled when the man moved swiftly and embraced her in her arms, a hug that was not void of warmth.

'You'll be going to Marondera. I'll be visiting your house often,' the man disentangled his arms. 'Both to see if you're a good manager and to receive your services.'

Panaka only nodded. Tears filled her eyes at the show of such extreme love and affection. She had never known that a simple hug could do such a thing as to melt the heart for she had never had the privilege of being hugged this closely especially from the opposite sexuality.

'It's a new house, you'll like it. I know you will, but first you'll go through the necessary training from Yemu here,' Kedha said eventually disengaging himself from the hug.

The door opened and a woman in a skimpy blue dress bound at the waist with a leather belt stepped in. She was beautiful beyond wonder and had shiny black hair that fell to her shoulders and a sensuous mouth. Her tread was graceful and firm as if she had been a model all her life and she moved her mouth, smiling and exposing two dimples that could do crazy things to the hearts of men. She was a woman few men would be able to resist and Panaka realised that her teacher to be was already several steps up the hierarchy of whoredom from a simple beautiful streetwalker.

'I can see you've already realised that you are going to be working with professionals,' Kedha was smiling as the girl Yemu came to stop in front of him in a seductive pose.

Kedha draped his hands around the girl's neck and told her. 'Take this girl and teach her the tricks of the trade. She's joining your team.'

'Welcome, Panaka,' the girl said warmly and embraced her. 'I know you'll like it here after the streets.'

'I hope so,' Panaka whispered.

When she left with Yemu, Panaka didn't know why she felt unhappy, except that maybe she had made a deal with the deceiver of mankind.

CHAPTER TEN

One Month Later

'How did you get to be here?' Panaka asked sitting on the bed. The air in the room reeked of the pot they were both smoking.

Yemu sat in front of the dressing table mirror putting on lipstick, in preparation for a night on the streets. She dabbed here and there at her face using a wet cloth. The girl waited until she had finished before she turned fully in her stool to face Panaka. 'I was a street walker in Bulawayo when I met Kedha and he invited me here.'

'What? You actually came here willingly?'

'It was not that willingly. These men are crazy. They visit areas where they know they can find people who will never be missed by society. They target mostly street children and prostitutes. When any prostitute goes missing people will think they've eloped or ran away with a wealthy client and with street children people, will think they've migrated in search of greener pastures,' Yemurai laughed at the last remark.

'What of all the captured boys, where do they go?'

'I heard Kedha owns farms abroad. Most of them are smuggled across the border to his farms and the others he sells to connections abroad, mainly in the Brazil plantations.'

'That's cruel of him.'

'Better watch your words and try to like it here. Don't ever think of fleeing, let alone report to the authorities. The man has Agents everywhere and friends in high places. Many who've tried that in the past all disappeared without a trace.'

Panaka sighed. 'I'll try to like it here.'

'Wait until you start entertaining men, then you'll see.

Have you been told what you're expected to do?'

'Yes, I'm to be a drug dealer and run a whorehouse.'

'Good. Kedha is always frank with people. If you had refused, he'd have ordered men to rape, kill and bury you.'

Panaka shuddered at the thought. Kedha looked exactly that kind of man. She had not been deceived by his soft-spoken voice and loving manner, for his eyes had told her a different story altogether. Beneath the veneer of education and soft living, she had seen in his eyes a man who could kill to protect his vast business empire, a man who could stop at nothing in order to achieve his objectives. 'How did you come to walk the streets?'

She saw a dark cloud pass over Yemu's eyes momentarily. It was there one moment and the next it had disappeared. 'I'll cut it short,' she said. 'I was a first born child in a family of nine. My father worked at a mine as an underground supervisor and my mother died after bearing our youngest sister. She was one loving woman and the whole mine grieved her death. For a time, my father looked after us. The trouble started when my father married again. I was fifteen then and as the oldest, stood up for my siblings' rights. My stepmother saw this as kind of a rebellion and began to punish me indirectly, for she feared my father. She would give my younger sisters and me less food than her own children and give me even less than everyone. I complained and she began to give me loads and loads of work. I told my father and he beat my stepmom for that. How I loved that day, hearing her cries for mercy and shrieking. Everyone laughed except her own children. After that, things became better and she kept her distance for seven weeks only to begin again with renewed vigour. Again, I complained to my father and the ritual was repeated again. My father loved his first wife very much and so her children. It was after that beating that things changed for the worst. My stepmom went away for several months with her children to her rural areas in Chipinge.

When she returned, my father suddenly fell sick. He spent nine agonising months on the deathbed, slowly losing his senses until at last he passed away, leaving behind some property. It was a pity that my father wasn't educated enough to leave behind a will and when we went to bury him in Hurungwe we returned to find the house void of property. Our stepmom had boycotted the burial and stripped the house bare. We did not know where she lived and when we had been living in luxury we had broken contact with most relatives and were not in good books with those that we knew. I presented my problems to a friend who told me that my body held the future of my younger siblings. She took me to the streets and I found fortune,' Yemurai paused staring fixedly into space before she went on. 'The greatest of the fortune came when Kedha kidnapped me and I agreed to all his terms. Now my younger brothers have grown and now work for themselves raised by Kedha's pay and my little sisters are getting married soon. They forgave me for being a whore because it was for them that I did it…'

'How long have you been here?' Panaka interrupted.

'About seven years.'

'That's a long time. Why don't you retire now?'

'Because only Kedha can tell you to retire when your beauty fades beyond his liking.'

'I see. Have you been working alone?'

'No. I had two partners who died recently.'

'Died, both of them?'

'Yes,' a gloom passed over her face again. 'I warned them, but they got carried away and didn't use protection. The disease came and ravaged them. Kedha ordered a mercy killing.'

Panaka's heartbeat increased. 'That is absurd!'

'It may sound so, but it happened. I now warn you my

friend. I went to school when my father was still alive. They talk about AIDS, it kills. Never entertain men without condoms. I have seen many who have died. I have heard the cries of the infected. Your path may not have crossed one with AIDS and pray that it will never. I have seen the results and I have heard their cries. I'll never do it without protection, never!' The girl was hysterical.

There was a knock at the door and a female face poked in. 'If you girls have finished, let's go.'

'We are coming,' Yemu said rising and taking her purse. 'Let's go, Panaka. Don't forget to pack protection in your bag.'

CHAPTER ELEVEN

The meeting room was a high ceiling library at Kedha's home in one of the flashier extremely low-density residential areas. It was a room designed with the greatest luxury in mind, a room where comfort had been preserved to detail.

The chairs were all leather, with leaning backs which were, but mattresses of utmost comfort in which even the average weighing man could be buried alive in the soft material.

The floor was heavily carpeted and all the furniture and antiques in the room were polished bronze. The unending volumes of books were neatly filed on the racks displaying to the visitors the calibre of man that Kedha was, a polymath.

In the room hung the aura and arrogance which only riches, extreme riches can achieve, from the fragrances on the clothes to the smell of fresh breath and the way in which the debate was being conducted, money talked.

Four men were seated comfortably around the room and Kedha was speaking.

'I think it is becoming risky with each coming day. Bit by bit, my neck is being exposed to the gallows. You must raise the stakes significantly or I quit and you look somewhere else for this labour of yours.'

'But still we go back to the fact that you are not going to much expense or pain to get the stocks because you are collecting them from where they are dumped on the streets and you give them a life at least. Not much risk and no loss to anyone,' the South African businessman said easily.

'But still the operation is planned and it can fail plus I pay the people who do the task,' Kedha argued.

'We have heard your argument my friend. You see, I acquired a new Estate recently, an extremely large maize estate, but the problem is with the labour. I depend on you now as I have done all the time. What we need is just a way forward,' the potbellied Zambian said drawing from a cigarette and blowing smoke into the otherwise clean air.

'We cannot up the stakes much,' the South African said.

'Then you have to look somewhere else,' Kedha said.

'No, no my friend,' the fourth man who had been silent said and all eyes swivelled to him. He shifted in his seat to attain a more comfortable seating position before he spoke.

'I agree with our Zimbabwean friend. The risk is just too high and with his position in the government, he has a lot to lose. I up my stakes to what he has demanded.'

There were grunts of disapproval from the South African and the Zambian as they looked at each other and shrugged.

'We agree then, but you must avoid selling us those weaklings. Most of them die along the way,' the Zambian said stubbing out his cigarette.

'I know, otherwise see you when I get the packages,' Kedha said dismissively as he laughed inwardly. As always, he had had his way.

'The courier is here, madam,' the short barrel chested man said through the half-open doorway to the woman who was seated in the bedroom. 'Show him in,' the woman said without averting her gaze from the magazine she was reading.

The woman was in her twenties, but she did not look it. She looked as if she were in her teenage years. She was neatly dressed in a skimpy mini and a dark shed of red lipstick was stuck on her mouth. Until one looked a second time, no one could recognise her for who she was, Panaka the ex-street girl now transformed into a young woman of elegant style and a fashion sense.

She looked up as the courier clumsily shuffled in. He was like all the others, dressed in a clean cut suit of foreign nature, a boy in his late teenage years with boyish features and an air around him showing that he somehow had passed through the streets and had been its citizen during a certain period of his life.

'What do you have today?' She asked even before he had gathered his breath enough to greet her.

'I've got some silver bullet pills and news,' the boy said eager to please.

'The pills first,' Panaka said ignoring the boy's excitement.

The boy took out a packet of pills and placed it softly on the woman's palm as if it contained eggs that might break on contact.

She took the packet and examined it on the light, opening it and dropping several into her palm as if they were prized gems. 'Then out with the news,' she said as if talking with the pills.

'A woman visited the stall today enquiring about you.'

'A woman?' Panaka was suddenly serious, 'What does she look like?'

'She's short, light in complexion, walks with a slight limp and has got one missing front tooth,' the boy grinned and added. 'But not so beautiful.'

'Shit!' Panaka snapped.

Even as the boy had been describing, the years had dissipated and she was brought back down the vista of years to the days of old, she sitting back and laughing as her mother danced grinning and exposing her missing front tooth. There was no doubt the description referred to her mother, every sense of her being screamed this. *How did she trace her from Mutare to Marondera?*

'What was she saying?' Curiosity got the better of her.

'That she was looking for a child called Panaka something

and that someone had spotted her on the stall some weeks ago selling her wares. Her description matched you.'

'Who did she ask?'

'Anyone whose face appealed. She thinks the girl is the owner of that stall.'

'Oh, I see,' Panaka moaned and she did see. She remembered the day she had spotted her mother's best friend waving at her through a bus window. She then had been sitting at a stall with some wares in front of her, pretending to be a vendor, but actually waiting for a drug dealer to contact her. It had been several weeks back and she had nearly forgotten the incident.

'You can go now,' she dismissed the courier.

The boy bowed, opening the door behind him, but before he could leave the bedside phone rang.

'Yes!' She answered.

'This Kedha, our South African contacts need more manpower, can you arrange for the procurement of it over there?'

'I'll see,' she said.

'I rely on you darling.'

'I know,' and the connection was broken.

She looked up at the boy who looked at her curiously, expectantly. It was hard to think that both of them had been living on the streets, though in different areas. Living on the streets always seemed to extract the worst out of mankind.

'Kedha needs more labour,' she said simply. 'So there must be a raid tonight.'

'That's good,' the boy danced.

The use of drugs had bred in Kedha's boy and most of his henchmen and boy soldiers a violent, almost sociopathic nature. Panaka thought for a moment. 'I'll be coming with you to join in the fun.'

The night was a dank cellar, home to a thousand evils, some that crawled, some that rolled, some that flew, but most terrible of all the horrors was the one that walked on two feet, an evil that was astray that night.

In the air hung the subtle perfume of pain and fear, both of which did not affect Panaka as she could have been during her own stay on the streets. She and the others had made their way from Marondera to Harare via cars. The van to carry the captured ones had followed, a huge metallic truck with no windows at the back whose inside reeked and bore the scars of tormented souls, hundreds of the young who had been kidnapped only to be launched onto the murky and treacherous journey into the unknown.

Beside her in the car sat Kedha's great recruiting man, the blue-eyed whip boy whom she now knew as Ngoni. Like her, he glanced straight ahead at the entrance to Eastgate's movie house where very soon the children would start to stream out. They would wait until the last departed then they would move in the shadows of Fourth Street to pick up the street children. They could easily identify them because they always lingered long after the others had gone, reluctant to move away from the house and the memories of a film still etched upon their minds.

Their comrades had already set traps around the kids' lairs. The doors of the movie house swung open and the groups of children streamed out chattering excitedly to each other. Even without ever having seen the movie, Panaka pieced together pieces from the gestures of the children narrating that it was a high adrenaline Martial Arts movie featuring one of those legends of oriental Martial Arts who never seemed to lose a fight.

The children quickly disappeared in groups and a group was left deserted in front of the house. Unlike the others, they were not chattering, but were murmuring in hushed voices. The doors of the house had been shut for the night. Panaka waited for the action to begin.

'We'll wait.' Ngoni said as if reading her thoughts. 'The first police patrol will come soon.'

He was right. They came on bicycles and the street children quickly vanished. The mounted men cycled after them shouting and cursing until the kids slipped through an alleyway where their bicycles couldn't follow and the officers just laughed and rode on.

'It must be now,' Ngoni whispered looking straight at an area where the kids had regrouped. Even as she watched, the pain and suffering of the unprotected began.

It was all triggered by the crack of the whip. The children reacted rapidly. They knew what the whip meant. They quickly scurried for cover only to be cut by another one in the eyes of Panaka.

It was like a scene from a film and she couldn't help giggling as whips found their marks and bodies wriggled. The raiders laughed and gave each other high fives, excited by the pain they induced. It was then that Panaka realised that the fear of Kedha was a trigger to the extreme sadistic acts from the boys. She felt elated at the violence and watched in fascination.

Ngoni nudged her and passed her a joint of marijuana, which she drew from deeply.

'Give me my own whip and I'll join in the fun,' Panaka said and climbed out into the action of naked cruelty.

The big room was once a farm warehouse in the town of Marondera. It was bare and dirty except for rows of chairs arranged around an empty space to form sort of a ring. In the chairs sat men and women of noble stature who laughed and chatted excitedly and in the open space stood two heavyset boys, facing each other ready to engage in a game of death, which both knew and feared.

Both of them had been on the streets, experienced the life there and had to some extent gave up on life, but not one of them was yet prepared to die and each wanted to prevent and elude its grip no matter what the cost could be.

'I place my bet on the toothless one,' Kedha whispered in his friend's ear.

'I bet on that tall one. Look how he oozes confidence,' the friend laughed.

A man stepped into the ring and bowed before the guests. 'Ladies and gentlemen, our last contestants are these two boys. One is from Mutare and the other from Harare. Now ladies and gentlemen, you can place your bets.' The man whispered to the two fighters who turned to face the crowd. From her vantage point, Panaka could see the faces of the fighters.

She gasped as she recognised one of the fighters. She instantly knew him from his ugly puffed up gorilla-like looks. It was Alifu, her former street partner and friend. The boy caught her eye and stared at her. She stared back, her face void of humanity. The appeal in his eyes was nothing to her. She saw the appeal turn to hatred even as the boy turned to face his opponent. He had realised she was now one of them she had become just like them, the infected, her hairstyle, her dressing, her smile and even the aura of arrogance that hung around her like a cloud of doom.

'The winning contestant will be branded only after the death of the opponent and the winner shall fight in similar fights and be spared the hard labour of the farms,' the master of ceremony said and stepped out. The bell rang and the fighters went for each other. The boy from Harare was fast and skill-less and Alifu the boy from Mutare was skilful and faster. The Harare boy attacked with such speed and ferocity that for a moment Alifu was caught off guard. A blow landed on his jaws and they gaped open to let fly some bloodied spittle. He spun in the direction that the blow had sent him and a left hook saved him from making a complete revolution.

There was a cheer from the crowd of Harare supporters and their boy began to jump up and down, hands raised in the on-guard position, a favourable fighting position.

'Fight, young man,' Kedha urged the boy he had transported from Mutare. Alifu moved his jaws. They were stiff, but no teeth had been loosened. The old fighter's instinct was awakened in him. The martial arts techniques in him were crying for release even as the boy came for him. He sidestepped easily and the opponent's fist sailed harmlessly past his head whirring in his ear, a sign that indeed this was a fight to the death.

Alifu gathered his strength and placed it behind the roundhouse punch that he delivered into the boy's stomach. He gasped as the punch bumped back, for the boy had tightened his stomach muscles into unbelievable tautness.

The Harare boy released a fist, a straight fist that smashed Alifu's nose flat onto his face. Blood splashed out in a scarlet fountain and Alifu shouted a stream of obscenities such that the crowd fell silent for a moment. The obscenities could have come from hell and even there could have shocked the father of all Evil, devilish proprietor himself.

The Harare boy came again at him, grinning murderously. He stepped short and his hands flew up to his groin. He had not seen the leg that had shot out in a deadly stopping straight kick. He bowed and an uppercut lifted him straight his eyes wide open as if in mock disbelief as shock waves of pain surged through his being.

There was an uproarious noise from the crowd and Alifu delivered an astonishingly perfect roundhouse kick and the boy from Harare fell amid much cheering. Alifu lifted his hands in triumph and Kedha shouted, 'Finish him!'

For a moment, the meaning was lost on Alifu and he continued pacing around the ring.

'I said kill him!' Kedha shouted.

Alifu stood rooted to the spot, alarmed. He had never killed and the words came as a shock. He looked at the Harare boy who was struggling to stand his hands on his groin. He hesitated.

'Kill him, Alifu,' a female voice said. 'It's you or him.'

He spun around to face the owner of the voice whom he already knew was Panaka. His eyes held hers and he felt a chill of awe. Her eyes were glazed and he instantly knew that she had not stopped what he taught her. She was high on drugs. '*It's you or him,*' the threat registered in the back of his mind and he bellowed as he flew for his opponent, delivering a mighty knee kick into the opponent's face. The Harare boy slumped onto the ground. Alifu knelt down over the boy, fists clenched in a fashion rehearsed over a lifetime of violence. He clubbed the boy on the floor, giving way to pent-up fury, screaming and shouting obscenities.

The MC stepped into the ring and stopped him. Alifu stood up and jumped with his knee onto the still boy's face. He felt the bones snap as he made contact and he stood up, breathing heavily. The boy was dead, but he did not feel triumphant as he was led away. It was only the instinct of survival amongst the greatest of odds that had led him to do it.

This was to be God's case. The other prisoners from the streets sped into the ring with equipment to wipe off the mess.

In one of the back rooms, which had been turned into a holding cell, Alifu sat with his head in his hands. The room was small, but when Kedha saw it possible it could hold up to ten people. Alifu was still alone in the room waiting for the other winners to be brought in the elite group who were to be warriors of war, who were to move around the country fighting for a cause that was nothing, but a product of greed and a lust for power. It was power from a date with human suffering, ill got and evil power, the power of a rat over a mouse the power of the rich to the destitute whom he made to lick his feet in order to satisfy himself.

The room was a total reminder of the barbaric side of mankind. It was as if it were a living mass grave and the misery of its ever mobile population was scarred everywhere, deep scratches on walls from fingernails gone mad constant sounds of terror hung in the air. Ghosts of screams and shouts, of false hope and silent dread. Alifu raised his head as the door opened and an expensive perfume wafted towards him preceding an expensively clothed woman whose face was unmistakable, but his mind was in strong conflict with the judgement that it was Panaka.

'Panaka, you are now one of them?' It was more of an accusation from one whose whole body ached from the activity in the fighting ring.

'As you can see it Alifu, it's the way it is and there's nothing I can do about it.'

'Why, Panaka, tell me why? I thought you'd been sold into slavery?'

'You were wrong, Alifu. Some are not sold into slavery. The girls are only given another shot at life, they are given a second chance at life another chance to live all over again. In fact, I personally was given an identity an identity in a world where it is the only thing that matters. Only the boys are sold. Life here is like heaven after the streets. It's like I've already reached Nirvana, the Buddhist state of bliss.'

'I can see you are high, Panaka. What's the substance?'

'Pure high grade marijuana. You taught me well Alifu. I'm

now a chain smoker.'

'On the streets I gave you drugs to soothe your sufferings, but stay out of the lawless acts, Panaka, please.'

'Don't worry about me, Alifu, worry about yourself for soon you will be leaving this country among baggage probably to fight for other men whose parents took life so seriously years back they probably sent their children to expensive schools in the hope that they become doctors or engineers only to discover they become something bigger than that. These men are great men Alifu, great men from the heart. Men who took life so seriously and maybe swore to call no man as Boss. These men give new lives to the lost, homes to the homeless and identities to the uncertain. They live beyond their names Alifu. Had I gone to school, then these men I would like to emulate.'

'I know Panaka, but even before I go there I have to tell you that I never thought I'd get the power to love in my life not even had I spared a thought to the word love even its meaning. Love to me was helping a comrade flee from the clutches of a rival or from the police. Not until the day you were kidnapped. I wouldn't eat for several days because I was worried about you.'

'You didn't eat?' Panaka laughed. 'Was it because of me or because you had nothing to eat?'

'Believe it or not, Panaka, but I'm also human. To be human is to be able to give love and to accept it in return. I love you, Panaka.'

Even in her world, Panaka hadn't felt any love before, not even a proper mother's love, but the powerful word registered in the deep recesses of her mind. Something stirred in her heart and her voice thawed, the ice in her voice disappeared.

'It's a pity, Alifu that you are telling me such things when the time has come to part. That time when the only thing both of us can say is goodbye in the hope that we meet in the life thereafter in a world where both of us may be engineers instead of poor street children.'

'But we shall meet someday, Panaka. I have a feeling that our roads will cross again. Promise me, Panaka, promise me that you'll hold me in your heart till we meet again.'

Alifu saw her hesitate, unsure of what to say and he added, 'In your eyes I see my future.'

'Alifu, I thank you for protecting me all those days in the streets, for striving to feed both ourselves,' Panaka was crying softly. 'Nothing, not even my love will compensate for that and besides, I've never experienced love before. I've never been a victim of love before so I'm not sure what I should be looking for...' a voice called her name outside the room in the passage and she went on, '... but I love you, Alifu. If I would stop your shipment, but it's beyond my power.'

'I know, Panaka, but I'm sure we'll meet.'

'I must be going. They're looking for me outside. Goodbye's not an option, don't say a word or I'll cry.' And she left the room...

Alifu took his head in his hands and slumped forward, his mind reeling on the verge of collapse, cursing his father, cursing his stepmom, his stepsisters for it was them he decided who had launched him onto this very dark and uncertain journey in life, they had removed his life from the rails of proper childhood and sent the train of his life plummeting into the murky waters of the unknown where everyone else feared to tread.

It was at this moment that some of life's lessons wafted into his mind, that each individual had to journey through a life that was different from that of everyone else and that no one could live for another person. He was beginning to decide that mothers were always the better parents because he doubted that had his mother been alive he could have suffered this much, but then again Panaka had suffered with her mother alive.

So did life need only both parents alive to see the children grow properly? Did the death of one parent and the introduction of a stepparent into the picture necessarily meant a bleak future for the child?

He knew that the answers to most, if not all, of life's questions lay only in those who had like him lived to experience such plights. Only those who had lived with stepparents could give true testimony of what it is like, the living testimonies that indeed such children can grow into respectable Ministers, engineers, doctors, nurses, pilots or teachers.

It dawned to Alifu at that moment how women are the only great weaknesses men cannot resist for had his father not been so seduced by his stepmom, then Alifu could have been a normal child like all the others of his age.

He was thrown out of his reverie by the door that opened and Kedha, the man himself, stepped into the room, the man Alifu decided was behind all this for it was written all over the man and the admission was in his eyes.

It was as if time stood still at that moment for a date between the street boy and the devil himself. So this must be how it will be like on the final day Alifu decided, people were wrong in their depiction of the devil. He was not always ugly and neither did he have any horns but was an ever-smiling being with power over other human beings deciding their life or death.

Alifu's mouth went dry. *What was he to say in front of the man he had loathed so much?* His eyes now held something for the man before him that was beyond hatred. There was awe in Alifu's eyes, awe for what a man this man before him was how much power he must be having to be able to command such a gathering as that he had seen cheering the fight.

For a moment, Kedha regarded the huddled ragged boy before him with a face void of expression before he spoke. 'Congratulations young man. You may never know how much you have earned me in bets today in the ring. You have made me richer than I was before. It is so because of your extra ordinary fighting skills that I have decided to keep you around here rather than sending you away to a fate unknown to anyone. You can be my fighter moving around and fighting in return for lots and lots of cash and some other benefits than you can ever imagine.'

Alifu looked disbelievingly at the man. *This really was happening to him?* He could not believe it, he actually earning money for himself?

The boy was lost for words.

'What is your name?' Kedha asked.

It was a question Alifu had dreaded for years. Did he still even have a name? He had nothing to show that he even had a name. He answered hesitantly, 'Alifu.'

'Your surname?'

'I do not remember it,' he answered truthfully.

'Then I will give you an identity young man. I am going to introduce you to a world that only days ago had been beyond your dreams. As long as you fight and win, you shall make a name for yourself and you shall be having everything that you require. Is that clear?'

Alifu nodded. This was to be the beginning of a life Alifu hadn't thought possible. Being called a someone and having many girls drooling at him as he won fight after fight. The whole idea was appealing. 'I will take it,' he said decisively.

'That is wise of you,' Kedha said. 'And besides, there is nothing for you in this world young man. Look around you,' he said motioning with his hands outspread. 'You have nowhere to go see, there is no one to love and no one to be loved by. You can see now that my way can be the only way you can take and only then you will cease to exist, but begin to live. What is living in this world if you never experience all these joys and luxuries of life even if you get the necessities? Living by necessities is only called existence and living by luxuries is life. The way you have been surviving on those streets is inhuman and you are at the risk of being judged never to have lived, identitiless? Who are you if you don't have an identity?' Kedha paused looking at the boy before him.

'You have just made a decision that will make all the difference in your life. The gap between fantasy and reality have been bridged by your wise and calculated decision and you shall thrive by virtue of your fists and fighting skills. You shall never live to rue this day for it is the turning point of your life.'

Kedha moved forward, patted the boy at the back and left the room.

Alifu began to see how every little thing one does in life matters. The martial arts lessons he had taken for granted when his father taught him had helped him on the streets and now had given him an identity

CHAPTER TWELVE

One Year Later

The atmosphere inside the car was tense, everyone ready, waiting, poised for what to three of them was to be their first assignment. The other one was several steps up the hierarchy of the unruly. The air inside the car was fetid and choking from the marijuana that had been smoked in the interior and from the sweating bodies inside the car that smelt like stale alcohol. They were bodies recently used to spending most of their time unwashed and smelling, the bodies of young men who had spent the greater part of their lives walking the streets of a nation neglected and forgotten.

Alifu was among the first timers and Dubz, another Zimbabwean immigrant who like Alifu had once walked the streets was the only one who had been in it for several times and more. The other two were South African locals.

Both new recruits were nothing unlike Alifu, orphaned children of the streets who had fought their way to the ranks of a prominent South African businessmen's *Death Squad* whose face they had never seen, but nevertheless served him with dedication because at least he had given them a roof above their heads, clothed them and fed them, but what really kept them going were the endless women and drugs that came with the package, an added bonus they had spent most of their lives fantasising upon, but previously beyond their reach.

This task was not very easy, the orders as they had come through the chief courier had been long and they had to be grilled into them, no mistakes were to be permitted.

They were seated in a silver Honda Fit watching the entrance to some fancy house in the leafy suburb of Lundi. The house inside was not visible from the road as a very tall durawall surrounded it and stretched for as far as the eye reached, as if the man who lived inside had erected it against all the rage of the world, to shut himself behind this impenetrable wall of stone and wire. It was as if he had known that one day men would come for him, men who held nothing against him, but who are soldiers of fortune, hired by his enemies to settle a score they knew nothing about.

This man, they had been told was their Master's political rival, a man who shared the same interests as their Master, who wanted to graze where their master grazed, wanted to trade where he traded and wanted to rule where their master ruled. It had been said that this man was the last barrier between their Master and a seat in the cabinet and whoever took him out would be awarded generously, there was always a nice bonus for snagging the prey.

The team that was assembled had been issued with AK47 riffles, teargas, balaclavas and petrol bombs. They were to take out the man and bring his empire crumbling to the ground so that not even his children would build anything from the ruins that would be left behind.

Alifu's mind drifted back to the day of his first entry into the South

After his briefing with Kedha, Alifu had been together with ten others loaded into a container of a haulage truck that went into South Africa. All gagged, bound and drugged such that they saw everything that happened, but couldn't act, their ears, open but couldn't hear a thing. It was as if turned into phantoms in this life, figures who knew no beginning nor ending, people who seemed to have forgotten even their own names. After that first numbing drug, a drug that Alifu and his friends didn't know was injected into bodies.

The drug had been administered by a woman whose gentleness had brought tears to all the boys in the container and she had whispered to them as she had administered the dose of immobility as the boys now called it. Her voice was soft and motherly and its sound had transcended time and all its meaning.

'Don't worry boys, this drug will make your passage to a new life bearable and less painful. It will cushion every jolt and every bump. Just know that Kedha is not an evil someone, but the giver of life to the hopeless, an apparition bearing a message on redemption, your manger, your hope and your guiding star. He will give you homes, identities and all your life wishes only if you serve him with unwavering loyalty. South Africa is very big, you need a generous supply of money to enjoy life there, and there are so many beautiful girls to sate your lust. All will be given to you, I promise,' she had waved when she was done and smiled as she left.

After that, the container had been sealed, leaving above them some breathing holes which helped them discern day and night, but no one cared whether it was day or night for they spent the whole journey in a haze as if in a dream and the air they breathed was thick and heavy and all were sweating as the sun bore down heavily onto the metallic container.

It took them three days to reach the city of dazzling lights and great activity which they had no way of knowing back then was Jo'burg, the great city of the South.

They disembarked during the night and could not help marvel at the lights of the city reflected in the waters of some dock where boats were moored. The breath of fresh air made them all cry.

It really was true that you will never know the value of what you have until you are deprived of it for some time.

They were taken to some huge house with a tall security fence with guards whose eyes were glazed and barely human, whom they feared and whose stares could wilt flowers. None of them had any way of knowing that very soon they too would be giving such stares and at that time, none of them had any way of knowing that these stares were a combination of brainwashing, drugs and the horrors these men had seen as they grew up. They had no way of knowing that these men too were once boys of the streets, rescued from a plight to be trapped in this life which masqueraded to many as the final refuge of the forgotten.

Weeks of training moulded out of the boys of the streets saboteurs and murderers, men who swore allegiance to some faceless men whom they regarded in their minds as the modern gods, for they had to be grilled and brainwashed to make out of them loyal servants.

They were trained to use knives, guns and in the deadly of all martial arts. They were trained to sell drugs and to transport them without arousing suspicion.

Dubz nudged Alifu as a metallic silver Mercedes Benz pulled out of the yard, driven by a man whose bulky frame was visible through the lightly tinted windows.

Everyone in the car fell silent as they savoured the beauty of the car that looked more of a sport than of a delegate type. It was a rare beauty in an area where money spoke volumes.

Too bad this is going to be the last time this beauty is going to grace the streets, Alifu thought to himself as they followed several yards behind the Benz.

They followed it for around fifteen minutes and it took a right turn into a narrow strip of tarred road that led to the estates of the Vaal where he owned some land.

It was at this point that Dubz stepped onto the gas pedal and put an indicator to overtake. The Benz gave way for the

Honda to overtake. The Honda came up level with the Benz and all the occupants of the Honda pulled down their balaclavas and fished out their weapons, aiming them out the windows.

The driver of the Benz, the bodyguard saw this and tried to accelerate, but he was several seconds too late. The blaze from Alifu's weapon caught him in the side and he lost control of the vehicle that veered off the road into a cluster of bushes, which quickly checked its further movement, and it came to a jarring stop.

The Honda came to an abrupt stop with the screeching of tyres and with an efficiency born of long and harsh experience, Dubz was out of the car and fished out a pistol from his belt. With several great strides, he was at the passenger side of the Benz where their target sat trapped by the inflated air bag. Dubz aimed for the head.

'Please, please,' the man's mouth moved in a silent plea to the boy before him whose eyes were glazed.

On the man's face was a look of helplessness and fear, a look that to any other person could have triggered some pity, but not to Dubz. He was not normal. He was a soldier under orders. There was no room for pity in his heart, for no one had pitied him in the five years he had spent wandering up and down in the streets of Soweto.

'Go to hell, big boy,' and he squeezed the trigger.

The shot echoed in the distance and the man's head exploded in crimson splotches. Dubz spit and ran back to the car where the other occupants sat ashen faced and sped off.

'My God, Dubz, you are efficient!' Alifu gave him a high five as they removed the balaclavas.

'Prepare a joint for me,' Dubz said as he accelerated away to the safe house, to report a job well done.

The visitor was casually dressed, a middle-aged man who sat

as if in his own house. He had fringes of white hair in his head. He had the wrinkled wizened face of a tired monkey, unless one looked a second time and recognise the lines for what they were, lines of an old age that was to the man coming faster than he could cope with for he still wanted to hold on to a past that was fast ebbing into eternity.

'How often do you do business in this town?' Panaka asked as she sat across the room from the man, her mini riding up to her thighs.

When she had seen the visitor, she had decided to handle him herself rather than sending one of the girls. She had recognised the man, but he hadn't recognised her.

'Not often, I live in the Eastern Highlands and am a clerk at a farm in Mutare. I only usually pass by on my way to Harare.'

Panaka nodded thoughtfully and stood up, letting the man savour her body. She had put on a slinky mini dress, bright with splotches of art deco colours, as though preparing for a night of abandon, but she herself knew she was close to breaking point.

'Prepare yourself for a night of total sexual abandon,' she laughed saucily. 'Follow me.'

The man stood up and followed, his own excitement building up. He glanced at the sign on the bedroom door that read. 'If you doubt feel sexy, stay at home. No one is forcing you.'

Panaka led him into the room.

It was the kind of room that could have been slotted into the Sheraton Hotel without anyone noticing the difference. It was comfortable, antiseptic and tasteless, decorated with the basic African non-taste that was not an international hotel style.

When they were inside, she locked the door and sat down on the bed. 'Do you want to perform it high or low?'

'Meaning?' The visitor raised an eyebrow.

'Do you take drugs before sex?'

The visitor shook his head. 'But if you like you can take.'

'Give me a second,' and she left the room.

The visitor looked around the room and his eyes came to rest on a photo on the dressing table. It was the photo of a young girl in her early teenage years. He recognised the photo. He had seen it several times on a wall in.

The door opened and Panaka stepped in and closed the door behind her. She saw the man staring at the photo on the wall. 'I see you have recognised that picture,' she said nastily.

'Panaka, is that you my daughter?' The visitor was surprised.

'Yes.' She did not try to deny it. 'Your stepdaughter, former I might say.'

'How much pain you caused when you left? Why choose to lead such a life, Panaka?'

'If I had not chosen this, where then would you have been getting your pleasure?' She laughed lighting a joint of marijuana.

'It's just that I felt lonely and…'

'You could have called my mother whom I know would have accompanied you with pleasure.'

The man shook his head, lost for words.

Panaka walked and sat on the bed. 'You were never a good father and neither were you a good husband to my mother. You loathed her because she had had me.'

'You are crazy, Panaka, I never…'

'No, I'm not crazy. It's the marijuana doing its tricks,' she laughed. 'It is the first time you have allowed me to do a nice thing dad. You gave me permission to smoke, to use drugs, that's wonderful. Had you been like that all along, then you were not going to face the fate that is going to befall you tonight.'

The man felt panic welling up inside him and knelt before his stepdaughter pleading, 'Please my daughter, don't try to do anything you will regret.'

'It is nothing I will regret father. At least maybe you will not live to see me regret.'

With studied courage, the man stood up. 'I am your father and it's you who is supposed to be kneeling before me not the other way round. I am leaving and if you dare stop me,' he glared at her and made the sign of a knife across his throat. 'You are a bitch just like your mother.'

'I will not try to stop you,' she laughed, her eyes glazed with an obsidian look. 'But they will.' She jerked a thumb at the closed door and it burst open. The man jumped back, startled.

'It seems the wheels of fortune have stopped spinning in your favour and unlike years ago, you are now at my mercy,' Panaka laughed.

The man stared at the three boys who had stepped in. They were all clean-shaven and good looking, but it was their eyes that frightened him. They were obsidian eyes, glazed and bloodshot, evidence of drugs. The trio stared unmoving at the man, their eyes void of humanity. Whips dangled at their sides.

'I am expected at the Marondera hotel in twenty minutes. If I don't show up soon, a manhunt will be set and all of you will be caught,' the man threatened, his voice reduced to a powerless shriek.

'Will they go house to house in all the residential areas asking for you?' Panaka laughed.

'Please, my daughter, please…,' the man knelt down again.

For an answer, the girl made a slight gesture and the crack of a whip tore the air. The man screamed out as pain seared through his back like a long razor cut with salt being rubbed in. He had never believed such agony was possible. He fell onto his back.

'That was for cheating on my mother,' Panaka laughed.

'Please, I'll pay, I'll pay!'

'I am not registered in any one of the provinces in this country and neither are they,' she gestured at the boys. 'We were all picked from the land of the forgotten and given identities, unregistered of course and no one will ever trace us,' Panaka stood up, 'Till we meet again father,' and she left gesturing to the boys.

For a moment, she listened at the door. There were gasps of pain as punches were delivered and hysterical cries aborted. These were punctuated here and there by the cracking of whips. She laughed to herself and walked away. The boys would kill him and clean the mess for it was their game. They would bury him where no human eye would ever lay a suspicious eye, in Kedha's private graveyard at the farm. Lesson had been taught.

Her phone rang and she answered it on the first ring.

'The woman has been spotted again, looking for you.'

'Kidnap her and bring her in,' she said easily and broke the connection.

'It can't be you, my daughter,' her mother shook her head, tears of joy wetting her eyes.

'It is me, mother,' Panaka was also weeping. When she had first seen her mother as she had been steered in, Panaka had been gripped by that instinct of every child and hugged her mother warmly.

'Why, Panaka, why cause all the hurt to me my daughter?' Her mother was weeping.

'It wasn't my fault, mom, was it?'

'So whose fault was it, Panaka, mine?'

'I think so, mother,' Panaka talked softly.

'How, my daughter?'

Panaka gestured to the boys who had brought her mother to leave and the boys left the two alone.

'I did not have an identity, mother. I was a no one, but I wanted to be someone in life mother. I was the laugh of the town, an unregistered child in a place where identities are something to go by. I couldn't live like that, not if I wanted to be someone in life.'

'Your father wasn't there to help my daughter. Besides, how many farm children live without identities? Hordes of them, the majority do, but only a few run away from home.'

'We are different, mother. That's ignorance and they'll continue living in the farms. Registration is a very important aspect in this country,' Panaka shook her head. 'I couldn't.'

'That is the past now, my daughter. Now that I have found you, I am happy that at last. I will rest assured. Let's go home.'

'Back to the farms?' Panaka laughed. She was feeling uneasy and she fidgeted. It was the result of having missed her daily dose of cocaine and pot. 'Excuse me, mom, just a minute,' and she left.

She came back after ten minutes and her mother looked up at her and frowned. 'You've been smoking?'

'Yes, mom. That's how I've managed to bear the years of identity-lessness here. You were asking me to go back to the farms?' Her eyes were glazed.

'We are now live in Morningside,' her mother said.

Panaka let out a laugh. 'You live in streets of Morningside?'

'No, your father is back and bought a big house in the suburbs.'

'He is back? As a ghost, the undead?'

'No, he is alive.'

She shook her head. 'My father is dead. It's a trick to let

me come with you. My father is dead. You described his death to me remember?'

'It was all just a hoax, Panaka. It was an excuse for marrying again,' her mother was hysterical.

'Then it's a hoax continuing,' she laughed.

'Please, Panaka, I know you are now on drugs. It is normal for one who has gone through a lot.'

'You are now considerate and understanding,' Panaka frowned, 'That's abnormal for you. It does not fit you.'

'Your father cried for me to bring you back to him. He had gone to work abroad, for you, but I did not understand that. I failed him, but he has accepted me back on one condition that I will bring you with me, to him.'

'So you divorced the farm manager?'

'I discovered that on his nomadic work with the boss, he was a whoremonger and he deserted me first because he was ashamed.'

Panaka became serious. The idea of seeing her biological father was tempting. She had become weary of running the whorehouses and playing hide and seek with the police. She had always dreamt of a decent life and a husband. This was a small fire in the middle of the desert, probably even a future. A new life was always appealing, free from all the fuss that follows constant watches for the law enforcers and constant fights with rival dealers. Panaka was tired of running and always having to watch her back. She had a dream beyond the whorehouse, the anticipation of a future where she would be the wife of someone and bear him lots and lots of children.

Her mother remained silent watching her daughter floundering in indecision. At last, the girl sighed and let the stub of pot drop to the floor and in a gesture perfected over a long time, she ground it with her foot without even looking.

'Mom, if I confess one thing, can you still accept me as your daughter?'

'I'll accept you, my daughter, even if you tell me you are the first woman Eve who brought sin and peril on this world. It is a wonder in life how sometimes it takes tragedy to teach us true love.'

'I ordered the murder of stepdad.'

The words did not have to, but they had an impact on the woman. She reeled with the force of it and her jaw hung open. 'You, you, you what?' She was shaking her head.

Panaka explained in-between her mother's sobs and the story was punctuated by her own emotions.

'You are my daughter still,' and they embraced, tears streaming down their cheeks, letting the warmth of forgotten love pass through them, strengthening the bond between them which no deed, no passage of time could ever severe.

The scene was all so emotional. 'And he raped me, mom,' Panaka said in-between tears.

'Why didn't you tell me then?'

'Because you always found me wrong in the end.'

'I'm sorry, Panaka.'

When at last they parted, Panaka's tone was business like. 'I am going to flee from this place and stop all this.'

'Let's go, my daughter.'

Panaka opened the door and led her mother out. In the doorway stood two boys who regarded them with glazed maniacal eyes. They were waiting as always for her orders.

'Don't lock the doors, I'm coming soon. I have to accompany my mother. She has found her prodigal daughter, but I told her I am being well looked after,' she forced a smile.

The boys did not smile back. They looked at her mother who shrank back even as the boys unknowingly opened the door for them to go out into the fresh air, free, to start a new life.

They walked away hand in hand to the bus station.

Panaka did not want to spend another night in town. She did one last act before boarding the bus. She called the police in Marondera, Mutare, Harare and Rusape, giving them descriptions of houses and farms that harboured child traffickers. As she climbed the bus, she knew that from now on she would not be ashamed to die. She had done something for humanity.

***

THE HERALD

Police in Marondera, Mutare, Harare and Rusape last week raided six farms and around twenty-four houses in the respective towns and released nearly two hundred children in the greatest case of child trafficking in the history of the country. It is believed that the children, mainly kidnapped from the streets were awaiting shipment to Zambia, Malawi and some other unnamed African countries near the Eastern Coast where they were to be sold as labour at the farms.

The children were found in warehouses, garages, attics and in the worst case, four were locked up in the boot of a car at one of the raided houses in Mutare.

The police, it emerged worked on a tip-off. Prominent Mutare businessman and Minister Mr Simbarashe Mukaronda known in the network as Kedha has been apprehended and is believed to have been the ring leader. The man was arrested at the airport whilst trying to make an emergency exit out of the country together with several of his top men in the network.

The Minister of Home Affairs, the Minister of Child Welfare and also several business people are asking the informant who informed the police to come forward to receive a cash reward of two million dollars...

The man looked up from the newspaper article that he had been reading. It was an article now fifteen years old and the man had fringes of grey in his thinning hair. He always read the article each time he found nothing to do. He had been among the children freed by the raid those years ago, but the painful memories no longer stabbed. Time had reduced them to a bearable throb.

'This article fascinates you, I see,' he had not heard his wife come beside him.

'Yes, I like it, but not more than I like you,' the man grinned, exposing his front toothless gums.

The woman set the tray of drinks down and sat beside her husband. 'It's the second best decision I've made in life, busting up that evil network.'

'And what is the best decision?'

'Marrying you of course,' she laughed and gave him a peck on the cheek.

'I think that was the best,' he laughed. 'Because you bought this estate and all the cars with money you were given as reward and also it accelerated your political career and your fight for children's rights.'

'You old loving fool,' Panaka laughed teasingly as she looked her husband in the eye and he returned the look, a moment of intimacy in which only the eyes spoke and each seemed to understand what the other person was thinking.

At that moment, like a long wrapped package, like wine that had been left for years to mature, the past unravelled before their eyes. In their minds individual events of the past began to interweave into a web of memories and they took on misty looks as they were taken back in time, plunged back to the years back and lessons from the past came into being, not just reminiscently, but with specks of the true world. Panaka's dreams, her words and everything began to have a new meaning, meaning which the eyes couldn't communicate and Panaka found herself speaking.

'Remember all the dreams that I had back on the streets Alifu? That time when I told you I had a dream that things will one day be right, do you remember? Do you remember that day I woke up crying because I had dreamt getting married? Do you remember that day I dreamt that I had outgrown everyone else and people were looking at me as a giant someone? As a someone in life. And do you remember what you used to say back then, that if wishes were horses then I would ride? Remember how you used to think that you would die on the streets and leave no legacy?' She paused.

Life is not like that, Alifu decided in his own mind. A person has two lives and that there is always a life stored somewhere in a person's life, a life which had to be unlocked to be lived and the key was always in the person's mind and failure to discover this key was the reason why one would die with the conviction that he had lived when he had instead only existed. For living according to his mind was experiencing all the lives set up for an individual, unlocking all the locked doors set up in one's life and leaving behind a legacy for people to marvel on as they look back on your life. Only then, Alifu decided could one have the honour of being said to have lived.

In his mind, he discovered that most people like what he did on the streets only existed as stepping stones and aids to the ones who would be living and their existence timed, the routine unvaried.

He in essence did come to realise that no matter what the circumstances may be, there was always a life out there waiting to be lived and unlocked and it needed only the person's initiative to live this sinister second life.

'Hi, mom and dad,' a voice said and they both turned to see their ten-year-old twins standing, holding hands. 'Let's go for a swim.'

Panaka looked at her husband who winked at her. 'We are coming,' she replied. 'Go ahead and tell the maid to fill the pool with warm water. I don't want you catching cold.'

'Thank you, mom,' they chorused and raced off, but one stopped. 'Mom, our teacher said we must submit our birth certificates if we want to participate in the swimming tournament next week.'

'Don't worry, dear, I'll drive you to school tomorrow and submit them. I don't want you losing them.'

'Ok, mom,' and she raced off.

'I wish I had grown up with such privileges myself,' Panaka said tears filling her eyes.

'Don't worry about your past. It was a lesson for you to carry through life. Now give your children all those privileges that you never got a chance to access so that they will never live to regret.'

'You are a darling, Alifu, I love you.'

'I love you too, my dear.'

'Do you remember that day long ago on the streets when I told you that things will be okay and you will live everyday like a holiday?'

Alifu frowned and suddenly smiled. 'Yes, I do, and you seemed to be prophesying then.'

'Right. I may be a prophet. So why don't we call up some street children and give them a big party whilst setting up a Children's Home of our own?'

'Go for a swim with the children. We'll organise for the party to be held next week,' Alifu patted her on the back and she stood up to go.

Alifu only smiled as he watched her go through one open eye. She was one woman who had made his life worth living.

It was all occurring to him now, all the lessons life had taught him, that it is only the best men and women on whom life had sent through a journey of ultimate test who became good parents. That only those whose early childhood held multiple scars, who having grown to be people undertook the greatest endeavours to see the betterment of their children.

It was then that Alifu understood the quote that said, *'Don't compare your life with others for you may not know what their journey is all about.'*

There were a great many people who could give anything to be in their place at the moment, but had they seen them years back they could have done anything to dissociate themselves from the couple. Few even now could believe that the couple had during a period back in time haunted the streets.

Alifu began to note that as we grow up it is those things that we are not privileged to have, those things that we long for, but cannot get that we in turn swear to give to our children no matter the cost. It was then that he discovered why most children outclass their parents. They unwarily are provided by the parents those things that the parents possessed only in their dreams. They always get the better from a parent who grew in poverty and yet many still grow to old age only to become another Kedha.

It was then that he learned to cherish each academic achievement of the young for he discovered that a community that can eradicate the scourge of *Children of the Streets* is only a community that has taken to heart the welfare of the child at a tender age, for the beginning and only the beginning can shape and mould a child's mind into an acceptable child of society or make them feel neglected, *outcasts* of society.

To him, Panaka had not met him by accident, but by appointment. She had changed his life. She had proved to him that it's never too late to have a happy life. Theirs was a very great from *rags to riches* story and they had followed the hard and dangerous way only to find gold at the end. They had boldly endured all weather, perils and life on the path. For them, it was destiny, that had sent them to follow the way of the streets.